BRIDE WANTED

DEBBIE MACOMBER

THORNDIKE
CHIVERS

This Large Print edition is published by Thorndike Press, Waterville, Maine, USA and by AudioGO Ltd, Bath, England.
Thorndike Press, a part of Gale, Cengage Learning.

The text of this Large Print edition is unabridged.
Other aspects of the book may vary from the original edition.
Set in 16 pt. Plantin.

LIBRARY OF CONGRESS CATALOGING-IN-PUBLICATION DATA

Macomber, Debbie.
  Bride wanted / by Debbie Macomber. — Large print ed.
    p. cm. — (Thorndike Press large print romance)
  Originally published: Don Mills, Ont. : Mira, 1993.
  ISBN-13: 978-1-4104-3760-0
  ISBN-10: 1-4104-3760-4
  1. Brides—Fiction. 2. Seattle (Wash.)—Fiction. 3. Large type
books. I. Title.
PS3563.A2364B885 2011
813'.54—dc22   2011004427

BRITISH LIBRARY CATALOGUING-IN-PUBLICATION DATA AVAILABLE

Published in 2011 in the U.S. by arrangement with Harlequin Books S. A.
Published in 2011 in the U.K. by arrangement with Harlequin Enterprises II B.V.

U.K. Hardcover: 978 1 445 83760 4 (Chivers Large Print)
U.K. Softcover: 978 1 445 83761 1 (Camden Large Print)

Printed and bound in Great Britain by the MPG Books Group
1 2 3 4 5 6 7 15 14 13 12 11

BRIDE WANTED

For Eric, Kurt, Neal and Clay
Macomber — the other Macombers.
Love, Aunt Debbie.

PROLOGUE

"Let me see if I've got this right," the man behind the desk asked Chase Goodman. He spoke around the cigar in his mouth. "You want to rent a billboard and advertise for a wife."

Chase wasn't about to let a potbellied cynic talk him out of the idea. He had exactly three weeks to find himself a bride before he returned to Alaska, and that didn't leave time for a lot of romantic nonsense. This was the most direct route he could think of for getting himself a wife. He was thirty-three, relatively good-looking and lonesome as heck. He'd spent his last winter alone.

Okay, he was willing to admit, his idea was unorthodox, but he was on a tight schedule. He intended to wine and dine the right woman, sweep her off her feet, but he had to meet her first. Although Seattle was full of eligible women, he wasn't fool enough to believe more than a few would want to leave the comforts of city life for the frozen north. The way Chase figured it, best to lay his cards on the table, wait and see what kind of response he got. He also figured this would get noticed by women who wouldn't necessarily look at newspaper ads or Internet dating sites.

"You heard me," Chase said stiffly.

"You want the billboard to read

BRIDE WANTED?" The fat cigar moved as if by magic from one side of his mouth to the other.

"Yes, with the phone number I gave you. The answering service will be screening the calls."

"You considered what sort of women are going to be responding to that advertisement?"

Chase simply nodded. He'd given plenty of thought to that question. He knew what to expect. But there was bound to be one who'd strike his fancy, and if everything went as he hoped, he'd strike her fancy, too. That was what he was looking for, that one in a thousand.

He was well aware that it wasn't the best plan. If he had more time to get to know a woman, he could prove he'd be a good husband, and God

9

willing, a father. He wasn't like a lot of men who could blithely say the things a woman wanted to hear. He needed help and the billboard would make his intentions clear from the first.

"I'll have my men on it tomorrow morning."

"Great," Chase said and grinned.

The wheels were in motion. All he had to do was sit back and wait for his bride to come to him.

ONE

Lesley Campbell glared at the calendar. The last Saturday in June was to have been her wedding day. Only she wasn't going to be a bride. The wedding dress hanging in the back of her closet would eventually yellow with age, unworn and neglected. Given Seattle's damp climate, the lovely silk-and-lace gown would probably mildew, as well.

Enough self-pity, Lesley decided, and with her natural flair for drama, she squared her shoulders. She wasn't going to let a little thing like a broken engagement get her down. Even losing money on the deposits for the hall and everything else didn't matter. Not really. Her life was full. She had good friends — really good friends. Surely one of them would realize the significance of today and call her. Jo Ann wouldn't forget this was to have been her wedding day and neither would Lori. Lesley couldn't ask for two better friends than her fellow teachers, Jo Ann and Lori. Both would have been her bridesmaids. They'd remember; no doubt they were planning something special to console her. Something unexpected. Something to chase away the blues and make her laugh.

Her mother and stepfather were traveling and probably wouldn't think of it, but that was okay. Her friends would.

The hollow feeling in the pit of her stomach seemed to yawn wider; closing her eyes, Lesley breathed in deeply until the pressure lessened. She refused to give Tony the power to hurt her. The fact that they still worked together was difficult to say the least. Thank heaven, school had been dismissed for the summer the week before and she had three months to regroup and recuperate.

Lesley opened her refrigerator and looked inside, hoping some appetizing little treat would magically appear. The same shriveled head of lettuce, two overripe tomatoes and a soft-looking zucchini stared back at her. Just as well; she didn't have much of an appetite anyway.

Men — who needed them? Lesley

shut the refrigerator door. Not her. She refused to become vulnerable to any man ever again.

Several of her friends had tested their matchmaking skills on her in the past few months, but Lesley's attitude was jaded. Whose wouldn't be?

The man she loved, the man she'd dedicated five years of her life to, had announced six months before their wedding that he needed more time. *More time.* Lesley had been incredulous. They'd dated their last year of college, gone through student teaching together. They even worked at the same elementary school, saw each other on a daily basis and then, out of the blue, Tony had insisted he needed more time.

It wasn't until a week later that Lesley discovered *more time* meant he'd fallen head over heels in love with the new first-grade teacher. Within three weeks of meeting April Packard, Tony had broken his engagement to Lesley. If that wasn't bad enough, Tony and April were married a month later, following a whirlwind courtship. Since she was under contract and her savings slim, Lesley couldn't just leave the school; she'd been forced to endure the sight of the happy couple every day since. Every school day, anyhow.

She worked hard at not being bitter, at pretending it was all for the best. If Tony was going to fall in love with another woman, then it was better to have discovered this penchant of his *before* the wedding. She'd heard that over and over from her friends. In fact, she'd heard all the platitudes, tried to believe them, tried to console herself with them.

Except they didn't help.

She hurt. Some nights she wrestled with the loneliness until dawn; the feeling of abandonment nearly suffocated her. It didn't help to realize how happy Tony and April were.

He'd tried to make it up to Lesley. He'd wanted her to assuage his guilt. Because they worked in such close proximity, there was nothing she could do but repeat the platitudes others had given her. For the last months of school, she'd had to make believe a broken heart didn't matter.

But it did.

The last time she'd felt this empty inside had been as a six-year-old child, when her father had arranged for the family to fly to Disneyland in

California. Lesley had been excited for weeks. It would've been her first trip in an airplane, her first time away from Washington State. Then, three days before the vacation was to begin, her father had packed his bags and left. He'd gone without warning, without a word of farewell to her, apparently without regret, taking the money they'd saved for the family trip.

Her mother was so trapped in her shock and anger that she hadn't been able to comfort Lesley, who'd felt guilty without knowing why.

As an adult she chose to forgive her father and accept that he was a weak man, the same way she'd decided to absolve Tony of the pain he'd caused her. It would do no good to harbor a grudge or to feed her own discontent.

Although it was easy to acknowledge this on a conscious level, it took more than logic to convince her heart. Twenty-one years had passed since that fateful summer, but the feelings were as painful and as complex now as they'd been to the little girl who missed her daddy.

When neither Jo Ann nor Lori had phoned by noon, her mood sank even lower. Maybe they were thinking she'd forgotten what day it was, Lesley reasoned. Or maybe they didn't feel they should drag up the whole ugly affair. But all Lesley wanted was to do something fun, something that would make her forget how isolated she felt.

Jo Ann wasn't home, so Lesley left an upbeat message. The significance of the day seemed to have slipped past Lori, as well, who was all starry-eyed over a man she'd recently started dating.

"Any chance you can get away for a movie tonight?" Lesley asked.

Lori hemmed and hawed. "Not tonight. Larry's been out of town for the last couple of days and he'll be back this evening. He mentioned dinner. Can we make it later in the week?"

"Sure," Lesley said, as though it didn't matter one way or the other. Far be it from her to remind her best friends that she was suffering the agonies of the jilted. "Have fun."

There must have been some telltale inflection in her voice because Lori picked up on it immediately. "Lesley, are you all right?"

"Of course." It was always *of course.*

Always some flippant remark that discounted her unhappiness. "We'll get together later in the week."

They chatted for a few more minutes. When they'd finished, Lesley knew it was up to her to make the best of the day. She couldn't rely on her friends, nor should she.

She mulled over that realization, trying to decide what to do. Attending a movie alone held no appeal, nor did treating herself to dinner in a fancy restaurant. She sighed, swallowing the pain as she so often had before. She was sick of pretending it didn't hurt, tired of being cheerful and glib when her heart was breaking.

A day such as this one called for drastic measures. Nothing got more drastic than a quart of chocolate-chip cookie-dough ice cream and a rented movie.

Lesley's spirits rose. It was perfect. Drowning her sorrows in decadence made up for all that pretended indifference. Men! Who needed them? Not her, Lesley told herself again. Not her.

She reached for her purse and was out the door, filled with purpose.

It was while she was at a stoplight that Lesley saw the billboard. BRIDE WANTED. PHONE 555-1213. At first she was amused. A man advertising for a wife? On a billboard? She'd never heard anything so ridiculous in her life. The guy was either a lunatic or a moron. Probably both. Then again, she reasoned, she wasn't exactly sympathetic to the male of the species these days. She'd been done wrong and she wasn't going to smile and forget it! No, sir. Those days were past.

Still smiling at the billboard, Lesley parked her car at the grocery store lot and headed toward the entrance. Colorful bedding plants, small rose-bushes and rhododendrons were sold in the front of the store, and she toyed with the idea of buying more geraniums for her porch planter box.

She noticed the man pacing the front of the automatic glass doors almost immediately. He seemed agitated and impatient, apparently waiting for someone. Thinking nothing more of it, she focused her attention on the hanging baskets of bright pink fuchsia, musing how nice they'd look on her porch.

"Excuse me," the man said when she approached. "Would you happen to have the time?"

"Sure," she said, raising her arm to glance at her watch.

Without warning, the man grabbed her purse, jerking it from her forearm so fast that for a moment Lesley stood frozen with shock and disbelief. She'd just been mugged. By the time she recovered, he'd sprinted halfway across the lot.

"Help! Thief!" she screamed as loudly as she could. Knowing better than to wait for someone to rescue her, she took off at a dead run, chasing the mugger.

He was fast, she'd say that for him, but Lesley hadn't danced her way through all those aerobics classes for nothing. She might not be an Olympic hopeful, but she could hold her own.

The mugger was almost at the street, ready to turn the corner, when another man flew past her. She didn't get a good look at him, other than that he was big and tall and wore a plaid shirt and blue jeans.

"He's got my purse," she shouted after him. Knowing she'd never catch the perpetrator herself, her only chance was the second man. She slowed to a trot in an effort to catch her breath.

To her relief, the second man caught the thief and tackled him to the ground. Lesley's heart leapt to her throat as the pair rolled and briefly struggled. She reached them a moment later, not knowing what to expect. Her rescuer was holding the thief down, and as Lesley watched, he easily retrieved her purse.

"I believe this belongs to you," her rescuer said, handing her the bag.

The mugger kicked for all he was worth, which in Lesley's eyes wasn't much. He was cursing, too, and doing a far more effective job of that.

"That's no way to talk in front of a lady," her hero said calmly, turning the thief onto his stomach and pressing his knee into the middle of his back. The man on the ground groaned and shut up.

A police siren blared in the background.

"Who called the police?" Lesley asked, looking around until she saw a businessman holding a cell phone. "Thanks," she shouted and waved.

The black-and-white patrol car

pulled into the parking lot. A patrol-
man stepped out. "Can either of you
tell me what's going on here?" he
asked.

"That man," Lesley said indignantly, pointing to the thief sprawled
on the asphalt, "grabbed my purse
and took off running. And that man,"
she said, pointing to the other guy,
"caught him."

"Chase Goodman," her white
knight said. He stood up, but kept
his foot pressed against the thief's
back as he nodded formally.

Lesley clutched her handbag to her
breast, astonished at how close she'd
come to losing everything. Her keys
were in her purse, along with her
identification, checkbook, money and
credit cards. Had she lost all her ID,
it would've been a nightmare to

replace. Nor would she have felt safe knowing someone had the keys to her home and her car, along with her address. The thought chilled her to the bone.

There seemed to be a hundred questions that needed answering before the police officer escorted the mugger to the station.

"I'm very grateful," Lesley said, studying the man who'd rescued her purse. He was tall — well over six feet — and big. She was surprised anyone that massive could move with such speed. At first glance she guessed he was a bodybuilder, but on closer inspection she decided he wasn't the type who spent his time in a gym. He had a rugged, outdoorsy look that Lesley found strongly appealing. A big, gentle "bear" of a man. A gym would've felt confining to someone like Chase. Adding to his attractiveness were dark brown eyes and a friendly smile.

"My pleasure, Miss . . ."

"Lesley Campbell. I go by Ms." She paused. "How did you know I'm not married?"

"No ring."

Her thumb absently moved over the groove in her finger where Tony's engagement ring had once been and she nodded. He wasn't wearing one, either.

"Do you do this sort of thing for a living?"

"Excuse me?" Chase smiled at her, looking a bit confused.

"Run after crooks, I mean," Lesley said. "Are you an off-duty policeman or something?"

"No, I work on the Alaska pipeline. I'm visiting Seattle for the next few weeks."

"That explains it," she said.

"Explains what?"

She hadn't realized he'd heard her. "What I was thinking about you. That you're an open-air kind of person." She felt mildly surprised that she'd read him so well. Generally she didn't consider herself especially perceptive.

Her insight appeared to please him because he smiled again. "Would you like to know what I was thinking about you?"

"Sure." She probably shouldn't be so curious, but it wouldn't do any harm.

"You run well, with agility and grace, and you're the first woman I've met in a long while who doesn't have to throw back her head to look up at me."

"That's true enough." Lesley understood what it meant to be tall. She was five-eleven herself and had been the tallest girl in her high school class. Her height had been a curse and yet, in some ways, her greatest asset. Her teachers assumed that because she was taller she should be more mature, smarter, a leader, so she'd been burdened with those expectations; at the same time, she now realized, they'd been a blessing. She *had* learned to be both tactful and authoritative, which served her well as a teacher. However, buying clothes had always been a problem when she was a teenager, along with attracting boys. It was only when she entered her twenties that she decided to be proud of who and what she was. Once she refused to apologize for her height, she seemed to attract the opposite sex. Shortly after that, she'd met Tony. It had never bothered her that he was an inch shorter than she was, nor had it seemed to trouble him.

She and Chase were walking back toward the grocery store. "You're a runner?"

"Heavens, no," Lesley answered, although she was flattered by the assumption.

As they were standing under the hanging fuchsia baskets, Lesley realized they had no reason to continue their discussion. "I'd like to thank you for your help," she said, opening her purse and taking out her wallet.

He placed his hand on hers, his touch gentle but insistent. "I won't take your money."

"I'd never have caught him without you. It's the least I can do."

"I did what anyone would have done."

"Hardly," Lesley countered. The lot had been full of people and no one else had chased the mugger. No one else had been willing to get involved. She'd received plenty of sympathetic looks, but no one other than Chase had helped her.

"If you want to thank me, how about a cup of coffee? "

Lesley's gaze went to the café, situated next to the grocery store in the strip mall. She'd just been mugged, and having coffee with a stranger didn't seem to be an especially brilliant idea.

"I can understand your hesitation, but I assure you I'm harmless."

"All right," Lesley found herself agreeing. Chase smiled and his brown eyes fairly sparkled. She'd hardly ever met a man with more expressive eyes.

When they took a table by the window, the waitress immediately brought menus and rhymed off the specials of the day.

"I'll just have coffee," Lesley said.

"What kind of pie do you have?" Chase wanted to know.

The waitress listed several varieties in a monotone as if she said the same words no less than five hundred times a day.

"Give me a piece of the apple pie and a cup of coffee."

"I'll take a slice of that pie, too,"

Lesley said. "I shouldn't," she muttered to Chase when the waitress left, "but I'm going to indulge myself." She'd forgo the gourmet ice cream in favor of the pie; later she'd drown her blues in a 1990s Meg Ryan movie, where love seemed to work out right and everything fell neatly into place just before THE END scrolled onto the screen. If ever there was a time she needed to believe in fairy tales, it was today.

"Sure you should," Chase said.

"I know," Lesley said, straightening and looking out the window as she thought about the reason she was pampering herself. To her embarrassment, tears flooded her eyes. She managed to blink them back but not before Chase noticed.

"Is something wrong?"

"Delayed shock, I guess," she said, hoping that sounded logical, and that he'd accept it without further inquiry. Funny, she could go weeks without dwelling on the pain and then the minute school was out and Tony and April weren't around anymore, she started weeping.

"It's just that today was supposed to have been my wedding day," she blurted out. Lesley didn't know what had made her announce this humiliation to a complete stranger.

"What happened?" Chase asked softly. His hand reached for hers, his fingers folding around hers in a comforting way.

"Oh, what usually happens in these situations. Tony met someone else and . . . well, I guess it was just one of those things. The two of them clicked, and after a whirlwind court-ship, they got married. They both seem happy. It's just that . . ." Her voice faltered and she left the rest unsaid.

The waitress delivered the pie and coffee and, grateful for the interruption, Lesley reached for her purse and took out a tissue. "My friends forgot that today was the day Tony and I'd chosen for the wedding." She sighed. "In retrospect, I don't know if I miss him as much as I miss the idea of the wedding. You know, starting off our marriage with this beautiful celebration, this perfect day. . . ."

He nodded. "And?"

"And I guess I became so involved in getting ready for the wedding that I didn't realize how unhappy and restless Tony had become. When he asked for time to think about everything, I was shocked. I should've known then that something was really wrong, that it wasn't just pre-wedding jitters. As it turned out, it was good old-fashioned guilt. He'd met April — Oh, we all work at the same elementary school," she explained.

"Teachers?"

Lesley nodded. "Anyway, he was attracted to April, and she was attracted to him, and the whole thing got out of control. . . . I'm sure you get the picture."

"Yes, I do. It seems to me that your friend's a fool."

Lesley laughed, but it sounded more like a hiccup. "We're still friends, or at least he tries to be my friend. I don't know what I feel — not anymore. It all happened months ago, but it still hurts and I can't seem to put it behind me."

"It's only human that you should feel hurt and betrayed, especially today."

"Yes, I know, but it's much more than that. Tony felt terrible and with all of us working together, well, that just makes it more difficult. I asked the school district for a transfer but when Tony heard about it, he asked me not to. He didn't think I should disrupt my life and why can't we still be friends, blah, blah, blah. The problem is he feels so guilty."

"As well he should."

"I knew I was making a mistake, but I withdrew the request." Lesley wasn't sure why she was discussing her broken engagement, especially with a stranger. It felt better to speak of it somehow, to lift some of the weight of her unhappiness.

Lesley lowered her eyes and took a deep breath. "Listen, I'm sorry to burden you with this," she said in a calmer tone.

"No, you needed to talk and I'm honored that you told me. I mean that. Have you been seeing anyone since? "

"No." Lesley sliced off a bite of her pie. "Lately I find myself feeling cynical about relationships. I'm almost convinced love, marriage and all that simply aren't worth the effort — although I would like children someday," she added thoughtfully.

"Cynical, huh? Does that mean you don't date at all? Not *ever?*"

"I don't date and I don't intend to for a long time. I'm not feeling very sympathetic toward men, either. On the way to the store just now, I saw the most ridiculous billboard. Some guy's advertising for a bride, and instead of feeling sorry for him, I laughed."

"Why would you feel sorry for the guy?" Chase asked. He'd already finished his pie and was cradling the ceramic mug of coffee with both hands.

"Think about it. What kind of man advertises for a wife? One who's old and ugly and desperate, right?"

"What makes you say that?"

"If he can't find a wife any other way, there must be something wrong with him. If that isn't cause for sympathy I don't know what is."

"You think the women who respond will be old and ugly, as well?" Chase asked, frowning. "And desperate?"

"Heavens, I wouldn't know. I don't understand men. I've tried, but I seem to be missing something. Tony was the only man I ever considered marrying and . . . well, I've already told you what happened to *that* relationship."

"In other words, you'd never think of dating a man who advertised for a wife?" Chase asked.

"Never," she assured him emphatically. "But my guess is that he'll get plenty of takers."

"The old coot's probably lonely and looking for a little female companionship," Chase supplied.

"Exactly," she agreed, smiling as she mentally envisioned the man who was so desperate he'd advertise for a wife. "Like I said, I couldn't even feel a little empathy for the guy. That's how cynical I am now."

"Yes, you told me you laughed." He paused. "You think other women will laugh, too?"

Lesley shrugged. "I don't know. Perhaps." Women like herself, maybe. The jaded and emotionally crippled ones.

"How long will you be in town?" she asked, deciding to change the subject. This conversation was becoming uncomfortable — and it wasn't revealing her in the best light.

"Another two and a half weeks. I can't take city living much longer than that. The noise gets to me."

"You've been to Seattle before?"

"I come every year about this time. I generally visit the Pacific Northwest but I'm partial to San Francisco, too.

By the end of my vacation I'm more than ready to return to the tundra."

"I've heard Alaska is very beautiful," Lesley said conversationally.

"There's a peace there, an untouched beauty that never fails to reach me. I've lived there all my life and it still fascinates me."

Lesley was mesmerized by his words and the serenity she sensed in him. "What town are you from?"

"It's a little place in the northern part of the state called Twin Creeks. I doubt you've heard of it. I won't kid you — the winters are harsh, and there isn't a lot to do for entertainment. By mid-December daylight's counted in minutes, not hours. By contrast, the sun's out well past midnight at this time of the year."

"Other than your job, how do you

occupy yourself in the dead of winter?" It fascinated her that someone would actually choose to live in such an extreme environment.

"Read and study mostly. I do a bit of writing now and then."

"I guess you've got all the peace and quiet you need for that."

"I do," he said. "In fact, sometimes a little too much . . ."

They'd both finished their pie and coffee and the waitress returned to offer refills. Lesley didn't entirely understand his comment, and let it pass. This was probably the reason he came to Seattle every year, to kick up his heels and party. Yet he didn't look like the party type. His idea of the urban wild life was probably drinking beer in a hot tub, Lesley thought, smiling to herself.

"What's funny?"

Lesley instantly felt guilty. She was being more condescending than she'd realized. Chase was a gentleman who'd kindly stepped in to help when all those around her had chosen to ignore her plight.

"Thank you again," Lesley said, reaching for the tab.

"No," Chase told her, removing the slip from her fingers, "thank *you* for the pleasure of your company."

"Please, picking up the cost of your pie and coffee is such a little thing to do to thank you for what you did. Don't deny me that."

He nodded, giving it back to her. "On one condition."

Lesley left a tip on the table, then walked over to the cash register and paid the bill before Chase could change his mind — and before he could set his condition.

"What's that?" she asked, dropping the change in her coin purse.

"That you have dinner with me."

Her first inclination was to refuse. She wasn't interested in dating and hadn't been in months. She'd told him as much. She wasn't ready to get involved in a relationship, not even with a man who was a tourist and who'd be out of her life in a few weeks. Besides, he was a stranger. Other than his name and a few other details, what did she know about him?

He must have seen the doubt in her eyes.

"You choose the time and place and I'll meet you there," he suggested. "You're wise to be cautious."

Still she hesitated.

"I promise I won't stand you up the way Todd did."

"Tony," she corrected. "And that's not exactly —" She stopped, amused and frustrated that she found herself wanting to defend Tony.

"One dinner," Chase added. "All right?"

Lesley sighed, feeling herself weakening. If she declined, she'd be stuck watching Meg Ryan and Tom Hanks in her sweats in front of the TV — and probably gobbling ice cream straight from the container, despite the pie she'd just had. The image wasn't a pretty one.

"All right," she said, with a decisiveness she didn't feel. "Six o'clock, at Salty's at Redondo Beach."

"I'll make reservations."

"No," she said quickly. "Not Salty's." That had been her and Tony's restaurant. "Let's try the Seattle waterfront. I'll meet you in front of the aquarium at six and we can find someplace to eat around there."

His smile touched his eyes as he nodded. "I'll be there."

Two

Chase Goodman stepped out of the shower and reached for a towel. He'd turned on the television and was standing in the bathroom doorway listening to snippets of news while he dried his hair.

He dressed in slacks and a crisp blue shirt, hoping Lesley didn't expect him to wear a tie. Gray slacks and a decent dress shirt was as good as he got. A regular tie felt like a hangman's noose and he'd look silly in a bow tie. He didn't usually worry about what a woman thought of his appearance, but he liked Lesley.

That was the problem. He liked her, *really* liked her. The hollow feeling hadn't left his stomach since the moment they'd parted. It was the kind of sensation a man gets when he knows something's about to happen, something important. Something good.

He liked that she was tall and not the least bit apologetic about it. He preferred a woman he didn't have to worry about hurting every time he held her. His size intimidated a lot of women, but obviously not Lesley. She had grit, too; it wasn't every woman who'd race after a mugger.

Objectively, he supposed, Lesley wasn't stunningly beautiful nor did she have perfect features. Her face was a little too square, and her hair a dusty blond. Not quite brown and not quite fair, but somewhere in between. Maybe it wasn't the conventional pale blond most guys went for, but it reminded him of the color of the midnight sun at dusk.

Her eyes appealed to him, too. He couldn't remember seeing a darker shade of brown, almost as dark as his own.

Chase was physically attracted to Lesley and the strength of that attraction took him by surprise. It confused and unsettled him. He'd come to Seattle to find himself a wife, had gone about it in a direct and straightforward manner. You couldn't get more direct than renting a billboard! And yet he'd met Lesley by complete chance. Not only that, his billboard clearly hadn't impressed her, he thought wryly.

Nonetheless, he wanted to develop a relationship with Lesley, but he was worried. Lesley was vulnerable and hurting just now. If he romanced her, even convinced her to marry him, he'd never be certain he hadn't taken advantage of her and her battered heart. Even worse, she might feel he had. Regardless, nothing could dampen his anticipation of their evening together. That was all he wanted. One evening, and then he'd be better able to judge. Afterward he could decide what he was going to do. If anything.

Sitting on the edge of the bed, Chase reached for the TV remote and turned up the volume, hoping the newscaster would take his mind off the woman who attracted him so strongly. Not that it was likely. Not with that swift emotional kick he'd felt the minute he saw her.

"Hiya, doll," Daisy Sullivan said, letting herself into Lesley's place after knocking a couple of times. "I'm not interrupting anything, am I?" Daisy lived in the house adjacent to Lesley's rental and had become one of her best friends.

"Sit down," Lesley said, aiming an earring toward her left ear. "Do you want some iced tea?"

"Sure, but I'll get it." Lesley watched as her neighbor walked into the kitchen and took two glasses from the cupboard. She poured them each some tea from the pitcher in the fridge. "I'm glad to see you're going out," Daisy said, handing Lesley one of them. "I don't think it's a good idea for you to spend this evening alone."

Lesley felt warmed at this evidence that someone had remembered today's significance. "The date slipped by Jo Ann and Lori."

"So what are you doing? Taking yourself out to dinner?" Daisy was nothing if not direct. Her neighbor didn't have time to waste being subtle. She attended computer classes during the day and worked weekends as a cocktail waitress. Lesley admired her friend for taking control of her life, for getting out of a rotten marriage and struggling to do what was right for herself and her two boys.

Her neighbor was a little rough around the edges, maybe a little *too* honest and direct, but she was one heck of a friend. Besides school and a job, she was a good mom to Kevin and Eric. Daisy's mother watched the boys during the daytime now that school was out, but it wasn't an ideal situation. The boys, seven and eight, were a handful. A teenage girl from the neighborhood filled in on the nights Daisy worked; Lesley occasionally helped out, as well.

"How does this dress look?" Lesley asked, ignoring Daisy's question. She twirled to give Daisy a look at the simple blue-and-white-patterned dress. The skirt flared out at the knees as she spun around.

"New?" Daisy asked, helping herself to a few seedless red grapes from the fruit bowl on the table. She held one delicately between manicured nails and popped it into her mouth.

"Relatively new," Lesley said, glancing away. "I've got a date."

"A *real* date?"

"Yes, I met him this afternoon. I was mugged and Chase — that's his name — caught the thief for me."

"In other words, Chase chased him."

"Exactly." She smiled at Daisy's small joke.

"You sure you can trust this guy?"

Lesley took a moment to analyze what she knew about Chase Goodman. Her impression was of strength, eyes that smiled, a gentle, fun-loving spirit. He was six-four, possibly taller, his chest was wide and his shoulders were broad. Despite his size, he ran with efficiency and speed. Her overall impression of Chase was of total, unequivocal masculinity. The type of man who worked hard, lived hard and loved hard.

Her cheeks flushed with color at the thought of Chase in bed. . . .

"I can trust him," Lesley answered. It was herself she needed to question. If she was still in love with Tony, she shouldn't be attracted to Chase, but she was. She barely knew the man, yet she felt completely safe with him, completely at ease. She must, otherwise she wouldn't have blurted out the humiliating details of her broken engagement. She'd never done that with anyone else.

"I'm meeting Chase at the Seattle aquarium at six," Lesley elaborated.

"Hmm. Sounds like he might be hero material," Daisy said, reaching for another cluster of grapes after she stood. "I've got to get dinner on for

the boys. Let me know how everything goes, will you? I'll be up late
studying, so if the light's on, let
yourself in."

"I will," Lesley promised.

"Have fun," Daisy said on her way
out the door.

That was something Lesley intended to do.

At 6:10, Lesley was standing outside
the waterfront aquarium waiting. She
checked her watch every fifteen seconds until she saw Chase coming
toward her, walking down the hill,
his steps hurried. When he saw her,
he raised his hand and waved.

Relief flooded through Lesley. The
restless sensation in the pit of her
stomach subsided and her doubts
fled.

"Sorry I'm late," he said, after dashing across the busy intersection. "I had a problem finding a place to park."

"It doesn't matter," Lesley said, and it didn't now that he was here. Now that he was grinning at her in a way she found irresistible.

He smiled down at her and said in a low, caressing voice, "You look nice."

"Thank you. You do, too."

"Are you hungry?" he asked.

"A little. How about you?" Pedestrian traffic was heavy and by tacit agreement, they moved to a small fountain and sat on a park bench. She didn't explain that her appetite had been practically nonexistent ever since she'd lost Tony.

"Some, but I've never been to the

waterfront before," Chase said. "Would you mind if we played tourist for a while?"

"I'd like it. Every year I make a point of bringing my class down here. They love the aquarium and the fact that some of the world's largest octopuses live in Elliott Bay. The kids are fascinated by them."

They stood and Chase reached for her hand, entwining their fingers. It felt oddly comfortable to be linked to him. They began to walk, their progress slowed by the crowds.

"Other than the aquarium, my kids' favorite stop is Pier 54," she said.

"What's on Pier 54?"

"A long row of tourist shops. Or in other words, one of the world's largest collections of junk and tacky souvenirs."

"Sounds interesting."

"To third-graders it's heaven. Imagine what their parents think when the children come home carrying a plastic shrunken head with *Seattle* stamped across it. I shouldn't be so flippant — it's not all like that. There's some interesting Northwest Indian and Eskimo art on display, if you want to walk there."

"Sure. Isn't that the ferry terminal?" he asked, pointing toward a large structure beyond the souvenir shops.

"Yes. The Washington State Ferries terminal. Did you know we have the largest ferry system in the world? If you're looking for a little peace and some beautiful scenery, hop on a ferry. For a while after Tony told me about April, I used to come down here and take the Winslow ferry over to Bainbridge Island. There's something about being on the water that soothed me."

"Would you take a ferry with me sometime?" Chase asked.

"I'd like that very much," she replied. His hand squeezed hers and she congratulated herself on how even she managed to keep her voice. Countless times over the past few months she'd ridden the ferry, sat with a cup of coffee or stood on the deck. She wasn't sure exactly what it was about being on the water that she found so peaceful, but it helped more than anything else.

They walked along the pier and in and out of several of the tourist shops, chatting as they went. It'd been a long time since Lesley had laughed so easily or so often and it felt wonderful.

As they strolled past the ferry terminal, Lesley asked, "Have you been to Pioneer Square? There's a fabulous restaurant close by if Italian food interests you."

"Great!"

"I'll tell you all about Pioneer Square while we eat, then," Lesley said, leading the way. The restaurant was busy, but they were seated after a ten-minute wait.

No sooner were they handed menus than a basket of warm bread appeared, along with a relish tray, overflowing with fresh vegetables and a variety of black and green olives.

"Pioneer Square is actually the oldest part of Seattle," Lesley explained, somewhat conscious of sounding like a teacher in front of her class — or maybe a tour guide. "It was originally an Indian village, and later a rowdy frontier settlement and gold rush town."

"What's all the business about mail-order brides?" Chase asked while dipping a thick slice of the bread in olive oil and balsamic vinegar.

"You heard about that?"

"I wouldn't have if it hadn't been for a TV documentary I saw. I only caught the end of it, though."

"The brides are a historical fact. Back in the 1860s, Seattle had a severe shortage of women. To solve the problem, a well-intentioned gentleman by the name of Asa Mercer traveled East and recruited a number of New England women to come to Seattle. These weren't ladies of the night, either, but enterprising souls who were well-educated, cultured and refined. The ideal type of woman to settle the wild frontier."

"What would Asa Mercer have said to induce these women to give up the comforts of civilization? How'd he get them to agree to travel to the Wild West?" Chase asked, setting aside his bread and focusing his full attention on her.

"It might surprise you to know he didn't have the least bit of difficulty convincing these women. First, there was a real shortage of marriageable men due to the Civil War. Many of these women were facing spinsterhood. Asa Mercer's proposition might well have been their only chance of finding a husband."

"I see."

Lesley didn't understand his frown. "What's wrong?"

"Nothing," he was quick to assure her. "Go on, tell me what happened."

"The first women landed at the waterfront on May 16, 1864. I remember the day because May 16 is my birthday. Seattle was a riproaring town and I imagine these women must've wondered what they were letting themselves in for. But it didn't take them long to settle in and bring touches of civilization to Seattle. They did such a good job that two years later a second group of brides was imported."

"They all got married, then?"

"All but one," Lesley told him. "Lizzie Ordway. Eventually she became the superintendent of public schools and a women's activist. It was because of her and other women like her that Washington State granted women the right to vote a full ten years ahead of the constitutional amendment."

"Now you're the one who's frowning," Chase commented.

"I was just thinking that . . . I don't know," she said, feeling foolish.

"What were you thinking?" Chase asked gently.

She didn't want to say it, didn't want to voice the fears that gnawed at her. That she was afraid she'd end up like Lizzie, unmarried and alone. These few details were all Lesley knew about the woman's life. She wondered if Lizzie had found fulfillment in the women's suffrage movement. If she'd found contentment as a spinster, when her friends had married one by one until she was the only one left. The only one who hadn't been able to find a husband.

"Lesley?" Chase prompted.

"It's nothing," Lesley said, forcing herself to smile.

The waiter came just then, to Lesley's relief, and they ordered. Their dinner was wonderful, but she'd expected nothing less from this restaurant.

Afterward, they caught the streetcar and returned to the waterfront. On the short ride, Lesley regaled Chase with the history of the vintage streetcars, which had been brought from Australia.

"This is Tasmanian mahogany?" Chase repeated.

"And white ash."

"I'm impressed by how well you

know Seattle's history," Chase said when they climbed off the streetcar.

"I'm a teacher, remember?"

Chase grinned and it was a sexy, make-your-knees-weak sort of smile. "I was just wondering why they didn't have anyone as beautiful as you when I was in school. I only ever seemed to have stereotypical old-maid teachers."

Lesley laughed, although his words struck close to home. Too close for comfort.

"How about taking that ferry ride?" Chase suggested next.

"Sure." Lesley was game as long as it meant their evening wouldn't end. She didn't want it to be over so soon, especially since she'd done most of the talking. There were a number of questions she wanted to ask Chase about Alaska. Normally Lesley didn't dominate a conversation this way, but Chase had seemed genuinely interested.

As luck would have it, the Winslow Ferry was docked and they walked right on. While Lesley found them a table, Chase ordered two lattes.

He slid into the seat across from her and handed her the paper cup. Lesley carefully pried open the lid.

"I've been doing all the talking," she said, leaning back. "What can you tell me about Alaska?"

"Plenty," he murmured. "Did you know Alaska has the westernmost and easternmost spots in the country?"

"No," Lesley admitted, squinting while she tried to figure out how that was possible. She guessed it had to do with the sweep of islands that stretched nearly to the Asian coast-line.

"We've got incredible mountains, too. Seventeen of the twenty highest mountains in the entire United States are in Alaska."

"I love mountains. When we're finished with our drinks, let's stand out on the deck. I want to show you the Olympics. They're so beautiful with their jagged peaks, especially at this time of night, just before the sun sets."

A short while later they went onto the windswept deck and walked over to the railing. The sun touched the snowcapped peaks, and a pale pink sky, filled with splashes of gold, spilled across the skyline.

"It's a beautiful night," Lesley said,

holding on to the railing. The scent of the water was fresh and stimulating. The wind blew wildly around her, disarranging her hair. She tried several times to anchor it behind her ears, but the force of the wind was too strong.

Chase stood behind her in an effort to block the gusts. He slipped his arms around her shoulders and rested his jaw against the top of her head.

Lesley felt warm and protected in the shelter of his arms. There was a feeling of exquisite peace about being in this place with this man, on this day. This stranger had helped her more in the few hours they'd been together than all the wisdom and counsel her family and friends had issued in months.

"Let him go," Chase whispered

close to her ear.

A thousand times Lesley had tried to do exactly that. More often than she cared to count, more often than she wanted to remember. It wasn't only her day-to-day life that was interwoven with Tony's, but her future, as well. Everything had been centered on their lives together. She couldn't walk into her home and not be confronted by memories of their five-year courtship.

The bookcases in her living room had been purchased with Tony. They'd picked out the sofa and love seat together, and a hundred other things, as well. Even her wardrobe had been bought with him in mind. The dress she was wearing this evening had been purchased to wear to a special dinner she and Tony had shared.

"I want to go back in now," she said stiffly, and wondered if Chase could hear her or if he'd chosen to ignore her request. "It's getting chilly."

He released her with obvious reluctance, and in other circumstances his hesitation would have thrilled her. But not now, not when it felt as if her heart were melting inside her and she was fighting back a fresh stab of pain.

"I'm sorry," she said when they returned to their seats.

"Don't be," Chase said gently. "I shouldn't have pressured you."

Lesley struggled for the words to explain, but she could find none. Some days her grief was like a room filled with musty shadows and darker corners. Other days it was like a long, winding path full of ruts. The worst part of traveling this road was that she'd been so alone, so lost and afraid.

The ferry docked at Winslow and they walked off and waited in the terminal before boarding again. Neither seemed in the mood to talk, but it was a peaceful kind of silence. Lesley felt no compulsion to fill it with mindless conversation and apparently neither did Chase.

By the time they arrived back at the Seattle waterfront, the sun had set. Chase held her hand as they took the walkway down to street level, his mind in turmoil. He should never have asked Lesley to let go of the man she loved. It had been a mistake to pressure her, one he had no intention of repeating.

"Where are we going?" she asked as he led her down the pier. The crowds remained thick, the traffic along the sidewalk heavy even at this time of night. The scents of fried fish and the sea mingled.

"Down there," he said, pointing to a length of deserted pier.

It was a testament to her trust that she didn't seem at all nervous. "There's nothing down there."

"I know. I'm going to kiss you, Lesley, and I prefer to do it without half of Seattle watching me."

"Aren't you taking a lot for granted?" she asked, more amused than offended.

"Perhaps." But that didn't stop him.

Not giving her the opportunity to argue, he brought her with him and paused only when he was assured of their privacy. Without another word, he turned her toward him. He took her hands and guided her arms upward and around his neck. He felt a moment of hesitation, but it was quickly gone.

He circled her waist with his arms and pulled her to him. At the feel of her body next to his, Chase sighed, marveling when Lesley did, too. Hers was a little sigh. One that said she wasn't sure she was doing the right thing.

He smelled her faint flowery scent. It was a sensual moment, their bodies pressed against each other. It was a spiritual moment, as well, as though they were two lost souls reaching toward each other.

For long minutes, they simply held

each other. Chase had never been with a woman like this. It wasn't desire that prompted him to take her into his arms, but something far stronger. Something he couldn't put words to or identify on a conscious level.

He longed to protect Lesley, shield her from more pain, and at the same time he was looking to her to end *his* loneliness.

Chase waged a debate on what to do next — kiss her as he'd claimed he would or hold her against him, comfort her and then release her.

He couldn't not kiss her. Not when she felt so good in his arms.

Slowly he lowered his head, giving her ample opportunity to turn away from him. His heart felt as if it would burst wide open when she closed her eyes and brought her mouth to his.

Chase wanted this kiss, wanted it more intensely than he could remember wanting anything. That scared him and he brushed his lips briefly over hers. It was a light kiss, the kind of kiss a woman gives a man when she's teasing him. The kind a man gives a woman when he's trying to avoid kissing her.

Or when he's afraid he wants her too much.

He should've known it wouldn't be enough to satisfy either of them. Lesley blinked uncertainly and he tried again, this time nibbling at her slightly parted lips.

This wasn't enough, either. If anything, it created a need for more. Much more.

The third time he kissed her, he

opened his mouth and as the kiss deepened, Chase realized he'd made another mistake. The hollow feeling in his stomach returned — the feeling that fate was about to knock him for a loop.

Sensation after sensation rippled through him and his sigh was replaced with a groan. Not a groan of need or desire, but of awakening. He felt both excited and terrified. Strangely certain and yet confused.

Lesley groaned, too, and tightened her hold on him. She'd felt it, too. She must have.

His hands bracketed her face as he lifted his head. This wasn't what he expected or wanted. He'd feared this would happen, that he'd be hungry for her, so hungry it demanded every ounce of strength he possessed not to kiss her again.

They drew apart as if they were both aware they'd reached the limit, that continuing meant they'd go further than either of them was prepared to deal with just then. Their bottom lips clung and they pressed their foreheads together.

"I . . ." He couldn't think of any words that adequately conveyed his feelings.

Lesley closed her eyes and he eased his lips closer to hers.

"I want to see you again," Chase said once he'd found his voice, once he knew he could speak without making a fool of himself.

"Yes" came her breathless reply.

"A movie?" That was the first thing that came to his mind, although it was singularly unimaginative.

"When?"

"Tomorrow." Waiting longer than a few hours would have been a test of his patience.

"Okay. What time?"

He didn't know. It seemed a bit presumptuous to suggest a matinee, but waiting any longer than noon to see her again seemed impossible.

"I'll give you my phone number," she said. "And my cell."

"I'll call you in the morning and we can talk then."

"Yes," she agreed.

"I'll walk you to your car."

He didn't dare take hold of her hand or touch her. He'd never felt this way with a woman, as if he'd lose control simply brushing her lips with his. All she needed to do was to sigh that soft womanly sigh that said she wanted him and it would've been all over, right then and there.

They didn't need to walk far. Lesley had parked in a slot beneath the viaduct across the street from the aquarium. He lingered outside her door.

"Thank you," she whispered, not looking at him.

"Dinner was my pleasure."

"I didn't mean for dinner." She looked at him then and raised her hand, holding it against his face. Softly, unexpectedly, she pressed her mouth to his.

"I . . . don't know if I would've made it through this day without you."

He wanted to argue with that. She was strong, far stronger than she gave herself credit for.

"I'm glad I could help," he said finally, when he could think of no way to describe the strength he saw in her without making it sound trite. He wished he could reassure her that the man she loved had been a fool to let her go, but she didn't want to hear that, either. Those were the words he knew others had said to her, the counsel she'd been given by family and friends.

"I'll wait to hear from you," she said, unlocking her car door.

He'd be waiting, too, until a respectable amount of time had elapsed so he could phone her.

"Thank you again," she said, silently communicating far more than thanks. She closed the door and started the engine. Chase stepped aside as she pulled out of the parking space and

stood there until her car had disappeared into the night. Then he
walked to his own.

THREE

The phone in his room rang at eight the next morning. Chase had been up for hours, had eaten breakfast and leisurely read the paper. After years of rising early, he'd never learned to sleep past six.

The phone rang a second time. It couldn't possibly be Lesley — he hadn't mentioned the name of his hotel — yet he couldn't help hoping.

"Hello," he answered crisply.

"Mr. Goodman, this is the answering service." The woman sounded impatient and more than a little frazzled.

"Someone responded to the ad," Chase guessed. He'd nearly forgotten about the billboard.

"*Someone!*" the woman burst out. "We've had nearly five hundred calls in the last twenty-four hours, including inquiries from two television stations, the *Seattle Times* and four radio stations. Our staff isn't equipped to deal with this kind of response."

"Five hundred calls." Chase was shocked. He'd never dreamed his advertisement would receive such an overwhelming response.

"Our operators have been bombarded with inquiries, Mr. Goodman."

"How can I possibly answer so many calls?" The mere thought of being expected to contact that many women on his own was overwhelming.

"I suggest you hire someone to weed through the replies. I'm sorry, but I don't think any of us dreamed there'd be such an unmanageable number."

"You!" Chase was astonished himself. "I'll make arrangements this morning."

"We'd appreciate it if you'd come and collect the messages as soon as possible."

"I'll be there directly," Chase promised.

Five hundred responses, he mused after he'd replaced the receiver. It seemed incredible. Absurd. Unbelievable. He'd never guessed there were that many women who'd even consider such a thing. And according to the answering service, the calls hadn't stopped, either. There were more coming in every minute.

He reached for his car keys and was ready to leave when a knock sounded at the door. When he opened it, he discovered a newswoman and a man with a camera on the other side.

"You're Chase Goodman?" the woman asked. She was slight and pretty and he recognized her from the newscast the night before. She was a TV reporter, and although he couldn't remember her name, her face was familiar.

"I'm Chase Goodman," he answered, eyeing the man with the camera. "What can I do for you?"

"The same Chase Goodman who rented the billboard off Denny Way?"

"Yes."

She smiled then. "I'm Becky Bright from KYGN-TV and this is Steve Dalton, my cameraman. Would you mind if I asked you a few questions? I promise we won't take much of your time."

Chase couldn't see any harm in that, but he didn't like the idea of someone sticking a camera in his face. He hesitated, then decided, "I suppose that would be all right."

"Great." The reporter walked into his hotel room, pulled out a chair and instructed Chase to sit down. He did, but he didn't take his eye off the cameraman. A series of bright lights nearly blinded him.

"Sorry," Becky said apologetically. "I should've warned you about the glare. Now, tell me, Mr. Goodman, what prompted you to advertise for a wife?"

Chase held up his hand to shield his eyes. "Ah . . . I'm from Alaska."

"Alaska," she repeated, reaching for his arm and moving it away from his face.

"I'm only going to be in town a few weeks, so I wanted to make the most of my time," he elaborated, squinting. "I'm looking for a wife, and it seemed like a good idea to be as direct and straightforward as I could. I didn't want any misunderstanding about my intentions."

"Have you had any responses?"

Chase shook his head, still incredulous. "I just got off the phone with the answering service and they've been flooded with calls. They said there've been over five hundred."

"That surprises you?"

"Sure does. I figured I'd be lucky to find a handful of women willing to move to Alaska. I live outside Prudhoe Bay."

"The women who've applied know this?"

"Yes. I left the pertinent details with the answering service as a sort of screening technique. Only those who were willing to accept my conditions were to leave their names and phone numbers."

"And five hundred have done that?"

"Apparently so. I was on my way to the agency just now."

"How do you intend to interview five hundred or more women?"

Chase rubbed the side of his jaw. This situation was quickly getting out of hand. "I'm hoping to hire an assistant as soon as I can. This whole thing has gone *much* further than I expected."

"If you were to speak to the women who've answered your ad, what would you say?"

Chase didn't think well on his feet, especially when he was cornered by a fast-talking reporter and a cameraman who seemed intent on blinding him. "I guess I'd ask them to be patient. I promise to respond to every call, but it might take me a few days."

"Will you be holding interviews yourself?"

Chase hadn't thought this far ahead. His original idea had been to meet every applicant for dinner, so they could get to know each other in a nonthreatening, casual atmosphere, and then proceed, depending on how they felt about him and how he felt about them. All of that had changed now. "I suppose I'll be meeting them personally," he muttered reluctantly. "A lot of them, anyway."

Becky stood and the lights dimmed. "It's been a pleasure talking to you, Mr. Goodman. We'll be running this on the noon news and later on the five o'clock edition, if you're interested in seeing yourself on television."

"So soon?"

"We might even do a follow-up report after you've selected your bride, but I'll have to wait until I talk that over with my producer. We'd appreciate an exclusive. Can we count on you for that?"

"Ah . . . sure."

"Great." She beamed him a game-show-host smile.

"Before you go," Chase said, gathering his wits, "how'd you know where to find me?" He'd purposely made arrangements with the answering service to avoid this very thing.

"Easy," Becky said, sticking her pad and pen inside her purse. "I contacted the billboard company. They told me where to reach you."

Chase opened the door for the two, feeling very much like an idiot. He should never have agreed to the interview. They'd caught him off guard, before he realized what he was doing. If anything, this meeting was likely to generate additional calls and he already had more than he knew how to deal with.

Chase slumped onto the bed. He'd tried to be honest and fair. He wanted a wife. For thirty-three years he'd been content to live and work alone, waiting until he could offer a woman a decent life. He was finished with that.

The shortage of women in Alaska was well-known, especially in the far north. When Lesley had told him the details about those Seattle brides back in the 1860s, he felt a certain kinship with Asa Mercer and the desperate, lonely men who'd put up the money for such a venture.

Lesley had told him Mercer hadn't had much difficulty convincing women to move west. That had surprised him, but not as much as the response his own ad had generated.

Lesley.

He'd meant to tell her about the billboard that first afternoon. But then she'd mentioned it herself and implied that anyone who'd advertise for a wife was crazy and pathetic. He'd been afraid she'd never agree to their dinner if she'd known he was that man.

He reached for the phone, intending to call her right then to explain. He fumbled for her phone number inside his wallet and unfolded it, placing it on the nightstand. After punching the first four numbers in quick succession, he changed his mind and hung up. This sort of thing was best said face-to-face. He only hoped she'd be more inclined to think well of him now that she knew him better.

He'd wait until a decent hour and contact her, he decided. His one hope was that she wouldn't watch the noon news.

Lesley woke happy. At least she thought this feeling was happiness. All she knew was that she'd slept through the entire night and when morning came, the dark cloud of despair that had hung over her the past few months had lifted. Her heart felt lighter, her head clearer, her spirit whole.

She wasn't falling in love with Chase. Not by a long shot. But he'd helped her look past the pain she'd been walking under; he'd eased her toward the sun's warmth. With Chase she'd laughed again and for that alone she'd always be grateful.

She showered and twisted her hair into a French braid, then brewed a pot of coffee. While reading the paper, she decided to bake chocolate-chip cookies. Eric and Kevin, Daisy's two boys, would be thrilled.

Chase might enjoy them, too.

She smiled as she held the coffee cup in front of her lips, her elbows braced on the kitchen table. No point in kidding herself. She was baking those cookies for him. Later she'd suggest an outing to Paradise on Mount Rainier.

True, Eric and Kevin would appreciate their share, but it was Chase she was hoping to impress. Chase she was looking forward to hearing from again. Chase who dominated her thoughts all morning.

The cookies were cooling on the counter when Daisy let herself in.

"Say, what's going on here?" she asked, helping herself to a cookie.

"I don't know. I felt the urge to bake this morning."

Daisy pulled out a chair. "It's the nesting instinct. Mark my words, sweetie, those ol' hormones are kicking in."

Lesley paused, her hand holding a spatula that held a cookie. "I beg your pardon?"

"You're how old now? Twenty-five, twenty-six?"

"Twenty-seven."

"A lot of your friends are engaged or married. You've probably got girlfriends with kids."

"Yes," Lesley admitted, agreeably enough, "but that doesn't mean anything."

"Who are you trying to fool? Not me! As far as I'm concerned, marriage and a family were the big attraction with Tony. He was never your type and we both know it. What you were looking forward to was settling down, getting pregnant and doing the mother thing."

"We agreed not to discuss Tony, remember?" Lesley reminded her neighbor stiffly. Her former fiancé was a subject she chose to avoid whenever possible with her friends, especially with Daisy, who'd insisted from the first that Tony was all wrong for her.

"*You* agreed we wouldn't," Daisy muttered, chewing the cookie, "but I'll respect your wishes as long as you fill me in on your date last night."

Lesley smiled. "Ah, yes, my date."

"You must've gotten back late. I didn't go into work at the bar yesterday because I had to study and I wasn't through until after midnight and I didn't hear you come home."

Lesley hadn't stopped to chat with Daisy, fearing that sharing her experience would somehow diminish it. She'd gone to bed almost immediately, wanting to mull over her time with Chase, put some perspective on it, luxuriate in the memory of their kisses.

She'd intended to think about all that. Instead, she'd fallen asleep almost immediately. Even now she wasn't sure how to interpret their evening together.

"Did you have a good time?" Daisy asked.

"Wonderful. We walked along the waterfront, and then went to dinner." She didn't mention the ferry ride. She couldn't. It was too special to share even with Daisy.

She didn't know what, exactly, had happened between them, only that something had. Whatever it was, she'd allowed it. Had participated in it, and in the end couldn't deny him or herself the pleasure of those kisses.

No one had ever kissed her the way Chase had, gently, with such infinite care, such tenderness. He'd kissed her the way a woman dreams of being kissed, dreams of being held. Trying to explain that was beyond Lesley. She had no idea where to even begin.

Daisy yawned with great exaggeration. "Sounds like a boring date if you ask me."

"Maybe, but I've never had two men fight over me with switchblades the way you did."

"Both of 'em were staggering

drunk. Besides, I had no interest in dating either one. After being married to Brent for five years, why would I want to involve myself with another biker wannabe? Charlie had the police there so fast my head spun. Good thing, too."

Personally, Lesley believed Charlie the bartender had a crush on Daisy, but she'd never said as much. He was a nice guy and he looked out for her neighbor, but in Lesley's opinion, his feelings were more than just friendship for a fellow employee.

"Don't sidetrack me," Daisy insisted. "We were talking about you and Chase. That's his name, isn't it?"

Lesley nodded. "There's not much more to say. I already told you I had a nice time."

"I believe you described it as *won-*

derful. You seeing him again?"

"We're going to a movie . . . at least I think we are. He mentioned it last night, but we didn't discuss the time. And he didn't say anything about it when he phoned a few minutes ago."

"So he's already called again?"

Lesley tried not to show how pleased she was. Chase had seemed distracted, but there was no disguising the warmth in his voice. She hoped he'd tell her whatever was troubling him when he picked her up that evening. He'd asked for her address and Lesley had no qualms about giving it to him.

"What's this?" Daisy asked, reaching across the table to a stack of mail and pulling out a catalog.

"A knitting catalog," Lesley said, putting the cookie sheets in her sink to cool.

"When did you start knitting?" Daisy asked, slowly flipping through the pages.

"A couple of months ago."

"Aha! The nesting instinct strikes again."

"Don't be ridiculous," Lesley said impatiently. She walked onto her back porch, retrieved an empty coffee can and filled it with cookies. "Here," she said, thrusting the can toward her smart-mouthed neighbor. "For Eric and Kevin."

Chuckling, Daisy stood and reached for the cookies. "I can take a hint. You don't want me talking about Tony *and* you don't want me saying anything about your hormones. It's downright difficult to carry on a conversation with you, girl."

After shooing Daisy out the door, Lesley made herself a sandwich and turned on the local noon news. She was chewing away when the billboard she'd seen earlier that week came on the screen.

Her interest was piqued, and she put her sandwich back on the plate.

The camera left the billboard to focus on the reporter who was standing below it. Lesley liked Becky Bright and the offbeat stories she reported. It was a compliment to her professionalism, as far as Lesley was concerned, that Becky Bright could cover the billboard story and keep a straight face.

"This morning I talked with the man who's so earnestly seeking a wife," Becky announced. "Chase Goodman agreed to an interview and . . ."

Chase Goodman.

Lesley didn't hear a word after that. His face appeared on the screen and he squinted into the camera and said he only had a limited time in Seattle and wanted to be as straightforward as he could.

Straightforward. He'd misled *her*. Talk about being unethical; why, he'd . . . he'd kissed her. He'd held her in his arms and . . . Mortified, she raised her hands to her face. She'd so desperately wanted to believe in Chase, but he was like all the other men she'd known. He was just like her father, who'd cruelly deceived her. Just like Tony, who'd broken her heart. Never again would she make herself vulnerable. Never again would she be so naive as to trust a man.

Never again.

"Your next appointment is waiting," Sandra Zielger, the attractive middle-aged woman Chase had hired that morning, announced. He'd been interviewing women all afternoon.

The first one who'd come was a pleasant woman a few years his senior who worked as an executive assistant for a big manufacturing company. She was congenial, well-educated and professional. When Chase asked her why she wanted to marry him and move to Alaska, she said she was ready to "get out of the rat race" and take life at a more leisurely pace. She'd been divorced twice, with no children. After ten minutes with her, Chase knew a relationship between them wouldn't work. He wasn't comfortable with her the way he was with Lesley.

The second interview turned out to be with a female plumber who'd been working in construction. She'd been out of work for three months and was looking for a change of scene. The first thing she asked was whether he wanted to sleep with her to sample the goods before making his decision. Even before he collected his wits enough to respond, she'd unbuttoned her blouse, claiming she didn't mind a little kinky sex if that interested him, but she wasn't overly fond of whips and chains. By the time he'd ushered her out the door, Chase felt shaken.

He wasn't sure what he'd expected when he'd placed the ad, but it wasn't this. He was looking for a woman with a generous heart, one with pluck and spirit. A woman with depth and sensitivity. A woman like . . . Lesley.

He rubbed the back of his neck, closed his eyes and sighed.

He tried phoning Lesley just to calm his nerves, but she wasn't home. He didn't leave a message.

By four, Chase had talked with so many women that their names and faces and stories had all started to blend together. Not a single one had strongly appealed to him. He couldn't meet with these women and not compare them to Lesley. They seemed shallow by contrast, frivolous and, in some cases, reckless. There were a couple he might've liked under other circumstances, and he'd kept their names and phone numbers, but not a single woman to compare to the one he'd met yesterday, quite by chance.

He glanced at his watch and knew he wasn't up to interviewing another woman. The suite he'd rented at the hotel was packed with applicants. Word had gotten out that he was in the process of talking to prospective brides and they were coming in off the street now. Sandra Zielger seemed to have her hands full, and seeing that, Chase intervened, escorting the husband-seeking women from the room with promises of another day.

"I've never seen anything like this," Sandra said, pushing her hair away from her face with both hands. "You should've brought some of your bachelor friends with you."

Chase closed his eyes and expelled

a weary sigh. "How many women did we see?"

"Twenty."

"That's all?" He felt the panic rise. He'd spent nearly an entire day meeting with women, and he'd hardly made a dent in the crowd.

"I take it you're finished for the day?" Sandra asked.

Chase nodded. He needed space to breathe and time to reflect. What he *really* needed was Lesley. He hadn't stopped thinking about her all day, or the kisses they'd shared. Nor could he forget how she'd felt in his arms. He wanted to hold her again, and soon.

He was halfway out the door when Sandra said, "You're not leaving, are you?"

"You mean I can't?"

"Well, it's just that there are a number of phone messages that need to be returned."

"Who from?"

"The radio stations, for one. Another TV station."

"Forget them. That last thing I need now is more publicity."

Sandra grinned. "I've had several interesting jobs working for Temp Help over the years, but I've got to tell you, this is the most unusual. I wish you luck, young man."

"Thanks," Chase answered. He had the distinct feeling he was going to need it.

Lesley had been filled with nervous energy from the moment she'd seen Becky Bright stand beneath that ridiculous billboard and say Chase's name. None of her usual methods for relieving tension had worked.

She'd gone shopping and fifteen minutes later left the store. She was too mad to appreciate a fifty-percent-off sale. That was an anger so out of the ordinary it surprised even her.

A long soak in the tub hadn't helped, either. By the time she'd finished, she'd sloshed water all over the floor and had spilled her favorite liquid bubble bath.

Even a fitness DVD didn't help, but then she'd stopped five minutes into the exercises and turned it off. If she was going to do anything aerobic, Lesley decided, she'd prefer to work in her yard.

She weeded the front flower beds and was watering the bright red geraniums with her hose when Daisy walked out of her town house in a pair of shorts and a Mariners T-shirt.

"You upset about something, honey?" she called, crossing the driveway that divided their properties.

"What makes you ask that?" Lesley returned in a completely reasonable voice. The fact that Daisy could easily see how upset she was fueled her already short temper.

"Could be 'cause you're nearly drowning those poor flowers. They need to be watered like a gentle rainfall —" she made sprinkling motions with her hands "— and not with hurricane force."

"Oh," Lesley murmured, realizing her neighbor was right.

"The boys thank you for the cookies."

"Tell them I've got a jarful they're welcome to, as well."

"I thought you baked those cookies for Chase."

"I never said that." Lesley was sure she hadn't.

"Of course you did, maybe not in words, but it was obvious. You like this guy and you aren't going to fool me about *that*. All I can say is great. It's about time you got over that no-good jerk."

"Chase isn't any better," Lesley said, continuing with her watering efforts, now concentrating on her lawn.

"What makes you say that?"

"You know that billboard off Denny Way that's causing all the commotion?" Lesley asked.

"The one where the guy's advertising for a bride?" It must have clicked in Daisy's mind all at once because she snapped her fingers and pointed at Lesley. "That's *Chase?*"

"The very one."

"And that's bad?"

"The man's insane," Lesley muttered.

"You didn't think so earlier in the day. Fact is, you were as happy as I've seen you in ages."

"That was before I knew. He goes on TV and says the reason he decided on the billboard was so he could be — and I quote — direct and straightforward. He wasn't either one with me."

"You've got to trust your instincts," Daisy advised, "and you had a wonderful time with him last night."

Now Lesley had heard everything. "Trust my instincts? I was engaged to a man who wasn't even in love with me and I didn't figure it out until half the school knew, including the student body." It still mortified her to remember the strange, sympathetic looks she'd gotten from her peers weeks prior to her broken engagement.

"Quit blaming yourself for that," Daisy said, placing her hands on her hips. "You didn't suspect Tony because you *shouldn't* have suspected him. Believe me, honey, you got the better end of that deal. Mark my words. Two or three years down the road, he's going to start looking around again. It's a pattern with certain men. I've seen it before."

"Tony's not like that," Lesley insisted. Even after all this time she couldn't keep from defending him.

She still wasn't over him, still wasn't over the loss of her dreams and the future she'd envisioned. She *wanted* to forget him, but it was hard. The first ray of hope had been Chase, and now that hope was dashed by his deception.

"It seems to me there's more to Chase than meets the eye," Daisy said thoughtfully. "You have to admit he's innovative."

"The man rented a billboard and advertised for a wife," Lesley cried. "That's not innovation, it's stupidity."

Daisy went on, undaunted. "He shows initiative, too."

"How can you defend him when you haven't even met him?"

"You're right, of course," Daisy agreed, "but there's something about him I like. He can't be so bad, otherwise you'd never have gone out with him."

"That was before I knew what he really was like."

"The guy's obviously got money. Did you ever stop to think about that? Billboards don't come cheap."

"Money's never interested me."

"It doesn't unless you need it," Daisy answered with a hint of sarcasm. "Another thing . . ."

"You mean there's *more?*"

"There's always more. This guy is serious. He isn't going to string you along the way you-know-who did. Good grief, you were with the-guy-you-don't-want-me-to-mention *how* many years?"

"Five."

"That's what I thought. Well, let me

tell you, there's an advantage in knowing what a guy wants from you. Chase doesn't have a hidden agenda."

"Everything you say is true, but it doesn't discount the fact that he deceived me."

"Just a minute." Daisy frowned at her. "Didn't you tell me Chase ran after the guy who stole your purse? It isn't every man who'd get involved in something like that, you know. Did you ever stop to think that mugger might've had a gun?"

Lesley had raced after him herself and that possibility had completely escaped her. Apparently it had escaped Chase, too.

"It isn't every man who's willing to put his life on the line in order to help another human being," Daisy continued.

"If the mugger had owned a gun, he would have used it to get my purse," Lesley said. That had just occurred to her. Now she was free once again to be furious with Chase. She didn't want to think of him as a hero, even if he'd gotten her purse back for her. The action had been instinctive, she told herself, and nothing more.

"I'm offering you some advice," Daisy said.

"Are you going to give it to me whether I want it or not?"

"Probably."

"Then fire away."

"Don't be so quick to judge Chase. He sounds like the decent sort to me, and more of a man than —"

"I thought we weren't going to

discuss Tony again."

Daisy shook her head as if saddened by Lesley's lack of insight into men. Her eyes brightened as she looked toward the road. "What type of car did you say Chase drives?"

"I didn't. Why?"

"Because a great-looking guy just pulled up in a red car."

Lesley whirled around to see Chase climbing out of it. His smile was tentative as his eyes fell on her watering the lawn.

"I haven't come at a bad time, have I?" he called from the driveway.

FOUR

"Hey," Daisy whispered as Chase approached, "this guy is gorgeous. You don't happen to remember the phone number on that billboard, do you? I think *I'll* apply."

Lesley cast her neighbor a scalding look.

Daisy laughed, obviously considering herself amusing.

"I take it you saw the noon news," Chase said cautiously.

"You mean the story about your crazy billboard? Yes, I saw it."

Chase took a couple of steps toward

her. "Are you going to squirt me with that hose?"

"I should." She figured it was a credit to her upbringing that she didn't.

Angry shouts burst from Daisy's house and Eric chased Kevin out the front door. Lesley's neighbor hollered for the two boys to stop fighting. It soon became obvious that she was needed to untangle her sons.

"Darn," Daisy said, "and I was hoping to hear this." She stepped forward and shook hands with Chase. "I'm Lesley's neighbor, Daisy Sullivan. Be patient with her. She'll come around."

"Daisy!" It irritated Lesley to no end that her friend was siding with Chase and worse, offering him advice on how to handle her.

"I'll talk to you later," Daisy said as she hurried over to her own house.

"I would've said something yesterday," Chase told her, keeping a safe distance between them. "But you mentioned having seen the billboard yourself, remember?"

Lesley lowered her eyes. She'd more than mentioned the billboard, she'd offered a detailed opinion of the mental state of the man who'd paid for it, never guessing it was Chase.

"You could have told me later, after dinner," she reminded him. "That would have been the fair thing to do."

Chase advanced one step. "You're right, I should have, but it completely slipped my mind. I got so caught up in being with you that I forgot. I realize that's a poor excuse, but it's the truth."

Lesley felt herself weakening. She'd enjoyed their evening together, too. That was what hurt so much now. For the first time in months she'd been able to put aside the pain of Tony's betrayal and have fun. Playing the role of tour guide and showing Chase the city she loved had been more than a pleasant distraction, it had freed her. But after she'd seen the noon news, all those reawakened emotions felt like a sham. Instead of anticipation, she'd suffered regret.

"I was hoping you'd agree to see me again," Chase said enticingly. "I've been meeting with women all day and I haven't met a single one I like as much as you."

"Of course you like me the best," Lesley said indignantly. "Only a crazy-woman would answer that ad."

Chase buried his hands in his pants pockets. "That's what you said when you mentioned the ad, remember? You had me wondering, but, Lesley, you're wrong. I've spent hours meeting with them, and that isn't the case. Most have been pleasant and sincere."

"Then you should be dating *them*." Her minuscule lawn was well past the point of being watered, but she persisted, drenching it. If she continued, it'd soon be swampland.

"You're probably right. I should be getting to know them better. But I'd rather spend my free time with you. Will you have dinner with me tonight?"

The temptation was strong, but Lesley refused to give in to it. "I . . . don't think so."

"Why not?"

"Something's come up unexpectedly."

"What?"

"I forgot I was meeting a friend."

"That's not very original, Lesley. Try again."

"Don't do this," she pleaded.

"Where would you like to eat?"

"I said I couldn't."

"Any restaurant in town — you name it."

Lesley hadn't expected him to persevere. But she could be equally stubborn. A rejection had already formed in her mind, when Chase removed the hose from her hand, putting it down. He took her by the shoulders and turned her to face him. She might've been able to send him away if he hadn't touched her, but the moment he did, Lesley realized it was too late.

She knew the exact second she surrendered; it was the same second she knew he was going to kiss her and how badly she wanted him to.

His palms framed her face and he took her mouth greedily. Not only did Lesley allow the kiss, but she assisted him. Her hands splayed across his chest and she leaned closer. His kiss was hungry and demanding, and she clenched her fists in the fabric of his shirt as she battled against the sensations and feelings that came to life inside her. By the time it ended, Lesley knew she'd lost.

"Do you believe in fate?" he whispered.

"I . . . I don't think so."

"I didn't until I met you."

"Stop, Chase. Please . . ." She was fighting him for all she was worth and losing more ground every second he held her.

"Dinner. That's all I ask. One last time together and if you decide afterward that you don't want to see me again, I'll accept that."

"Promise?"

"Cross my heart and hope to die."

Despite her indecision, Lesley had to laugh. That sounded like something the kids next door would say.

"Now, where would you like to eat? Anyplace in town, just name it."

"Ah . . ."

"The Space Needle? Canlis? Il Bistro?"

Lesley could suggest a better way of testing a man's character than sitting across from him in some fancy restaurant with a bevy of attentive waiters seeing to their every need.

"I'd like to eat at Bobby's Burgers and then play a game of golf."

Chase's eyes widened. "Golf?"

"You heard me."

"Lesley, I don't know if you realize this, but there isn't a golf course within eight hundred miles of Twin Creeks. I've never played the game."

"You'll pick it up fast, I'm sure. Anyway, those are my conditions. Take them or leave them."

Chase groaned. "All right, if you want to see me make a fool of myself."

Miniature golf. That was what Lesley had in mind.

She'd left him worrying all the way through their hamburgers before they drove to the golf course and he learned the truth. It was a just punishment, he decided, for what he'd put her through.

He'd suspected Lesley would be good at it and she was, soundly defeating him on the first nine holes. But as she'd said, he was a fast learner, rallying on the last nine. When they added up their scores, Lesley won by three strokes.

"I can't remember the last time I laughed so much," she said over a glass of iced tea. They were relaxing on the patio under a pink-and-orange-striped umbrella, surrounded by children and a handful of adults. "You're a good sport, Chase."

"Does that surprise you?"

She hesitated. "A little. Men don't like to lose, especially to a woman."

"That's not true in all situations, just some."

"Name one." Her challenge was there, bold and unmistakable.

"When it comes to a woman deciding between two men," he said thoughtfully. "Naturally, I can't speak for all men, but there's one thing that bothers me more than anything."

"And that's?"

"When I'm forced to compete with another man for a woman's affection."

Lesley grew quiet after that, and Chase hoped he hadn't offended her with his honesty. He couldn't apologize for speaking the truth.

"Tell me about the women you saw today," she said unexpectedly, sounding almost cheerful. He caught the gleam in her eye and realized she was prepared to hear horror stories.

"I was really surprised by some," he began.

"Oh? Were they that awful?"

"No." He shook his head. "Not at all — there were some classy women in the group, with good educations. One of the first few I interviewed had her master's degree."

"What prompted *her* to respond to your ad?" The self-satisfied look disappeared, replaced by one of genuine curiosity.

Chase had wondered about that himself. "I asked about her motives right off. Don't get me wrong — Twin Creeks is a nice, civilized town, but it's a long way from shopping centers, large libraries and cultural events. Granted, we have TV and the Internet, but you aren't ever going to see any Broadway shows performed there. I explained all that to Christine."

"And she still wanted to marry you?"

Chase nodded. "At least she said she did. She explained that she's in her late thirties and has a successful career. But now she realizes how badly she wants a husband and family. She claimed every guy she's dated in the last few years is emotionally scarred from a breakup or a divorce."

"Having reentered the dating scene myself, I'm beginning to see how true that is."

"Christine is mainly interested in starting a family," Chase concluded.

"How do you feel about children?" She propped her elbows on the table and rested her chin in her palms as she studied him.

"I want a family, but I'd prefer to wait a year or two, to give my wife the opportunity to know me better and for me to know her. In my view, it's important to be sure the marriage is going to last before we bring a child into the equation."

"That's an intelligent way of looking at it."

Lesley went silent again and he saw pain in her eyes and wondered at the cause. He was about to question her when she spoke again.

"Other than Christine, is there another woman who made an impression on you?"

"Several. A female plumber who let me know she doesn't, uh, mind kinky sex."

The look that came over Lesley was

very prim and proper. "I see."

"And Bunny, who has four children under the age of six."

"Oh, my goodness."

"She was looking for someone to help her raise her kids and was honest about it. Her ex-husband abandoned them nine months ago."

"The creep."

Chase agreed with her. "I don't understand how a man can walk away from his responsibilities like that. What he did to Bunny is bad enough, but to leave those beautiful children . . ."

"She brought them?"

"No, I asked to see a picture. They're cute as could be. I felt sorry for her." He didn't mention that he'd given her enough money to fill her gas tank so she could get home and paid for a week's worth of groceries. She hadn't asked, but he could tell she was in dire financial straits.

"You aren't interested in a woman with excess baggage?" she asked, almost flippantly. Though he'd only known Lesley a short time, he already knew it wasn't like her to be so offhand. He suspected something else was bothering her.

"Bunny's a good woman who didn't deserve to be treated so badly by the man she'd loved and trusted. The divorce was final less than a week ago. Bunny, and the children, too, need more love and help than I could give them. To answer your question, no, I don't object to marrying a woman with children."

Lesley was silent for a long time after that. "My dad left us," she finally said in a small voice.

Chase chose his words carefully, not knowing how to comment or if he should. "It must have been very hard."

"I was only six and we were going to Disneyland. Mom had worked a second job in order to save extra money for the trip. Dad took the money when he left."

"Oh, Lesley, I'm sorry."

The look in her eyes became distant, as if she were that six-year-old child, reliving the nightmare of being abandoned by her father all over again.

"I know I shouldn't have blamed myself. I didn't drive my father away, but for years I was convinced that if I'd been the son he wanted, he'd never have left."

"Have you had any contact with him since?"

"He called when I was fifteen and wanted to see me."

"Did you?"

She nodded. "After being so bitterly hurt, I didn't have a lot of hope for our meeting. It's funny the things a child will remember about someone. I always thought of my dad as big and strong and invincible. When we met again nine years later, I realized he was weak and selfish. We had lunch together and he told me I could order anything I wanted. I remember I asked for the most expensive thing on the menu even though I didn't like steak. I barely touched the steak sandwich and took it home for our dog. I made sure he knew he'd paid top dollar to feed our collie, too."

"What made him contact you after all those years?"

Lesley sighed. "He seemed to want me to absolve him from his guilt. He told me how hard his life had been when he was married to my mother and had a child — me — with all the responsibilities that entails. He claimed he'd married too young, that they'd both made mistakes. He said he couldn't handle the pressures of constantly being in debt and never having money to do the kinds of things he wanted to do.

"That's when I learned the truth. My dad walked out on my mother and me because he wanted to race sports cars. Imagine, driving a sports car meaning more to him than his wife and daughter.

"You might think badly of me, but

I wouldn't give him the forgiveness he was seeking — not then. It wasn't until later, in my early twenties, when I learned he'd died of cancer, that I was able to find it in my heart to forgive him."

"I don't know how any fifteen-year-old could have forgiven someone who'd wounded her so deeply," Chase said, reaching for her hand. She gripped his fingers with surprising strength and intuitively Chase knew she didn't often share this painful part of her childhood.

She offered him a brief smile and picked up her drink.

"Did your mother ever remarry?"

"Yes," Lesley answered, "to a wonderful man who's perfect for her. You'd have to meet my mother to understand. She has a tendency to be something of a curmudgeon. It took her a long time to find the courage to commit herself to another relationship.

"I was out of high school before she married Ken, although they'd dated for years. She never told me this, but my guess is that Ken said either they marry or end the relationship. I don't think he would've followed through on the threat, but it worked.

"He and Mom are both retired. They live on a small ranch in Montana now and really love it."

"They sound happy."

"They'd like a couple of grandkids to spoil someday but —" Lesley stopped abruptly and her face turned a soft shade of pink.

"But what?" he inquired.

"Oh, nothing." She shrugged, looking decidedly uncomfortable. "It's just something Daisy said to me this afternoon. And . . . she might be right." Her voice faded.

"Right about what?"

"Nothing," she said quickly.

Whatever the subject, it was obvious that Lesley wasn't going to discuss it with him.

"Will you be meeting more women tomorrow?" Lesley asked.

Chase nodded with little enthusiasm. "I should never have agreed to that news story. The phones have been ringing off the hook ever since. There's no way I could possibly interview eight hundred women in two weeks' time."

"Eight hundred!"

Lesley sounded as shocked as he'd been when he'd heard the original number of five hundred. Since the story had aired, three hundred additional calls had poured in.

"That's . . . incredible."

"Just remember, I haven't met a single one I like better than you."

Lesley laughed. "You've already heard my answer to that."

"I don't have much time in Seattle, Lesley. Less than three weeks. I need to make some decisions soon. If you'd be willing to marry me, I'd promise to be a good husband to you."

"Hold it!" she said, raising both hands. "Back up. I'm not in the market for a husband. Not now and possibly never again. Men have done some real damage to my heart, starting with my father and most recently Tony. I don't need a man in my life."

"True, but do you *want* one?"

She hesitated. "I don't know."

"It's something to think about, then, isn't it?"

"Not right now," she answered, her voice insistent. "I don't want to consider anything but having fun. That's my goal for this summer. I want to put the past behind me and get on with life in a positive way."

"I do, too," Chase assured her, and it was true in a more profound way than she probably realized.

"I baked cookies this morning," she said. "It was the first time in months I've wanted to bake anything."

"I don't suppose you saved any for me?"

Lesley smiled as if she knew something he didn't. "There's a full cookie jar reserved for you." She suddenly recalled that she'd said Kevin and Eric could have them. She'd have to compromise. "Well, half a cookie jar," she amended.

Chase couldn't remember the last time he'd tasted home-baked cookies. "This calls for a picnic, don't you think?"

"Paradise."

He frowned. "Do I have to wait that long to try these cookies of yours?"

"No, silly. Paradise is in the national park on Mount Rainier. There's a lodge there and several trails and fields of wildflowers so abundant, they'll take your breath away."

"Sounds like Alaska."

"It's one of my favorite places in the world."

"Let's go, then. We'll leave first thing in the morning."

"You can't," she said, with a superior look.

"Why can't I?"

"Because you'll be interviewing a prospective wife. Eight hundred prospective wives to be exact."

Chase cursed under his breath and Lesley burst out laughing. Only then did Chase see any amusement in his predicament. What she didn't seem to understand, and what he was going to have to prove, was that he'd willingly leave all eight hundred prospects behind in order to spend time with *her.*

The sun had barely peeked over the horizon when Chase arrived. Lesley had been up for an hour, packing their lunch and preparing for their day. Her hiking boots and a sweater were in a knapsack by the door and the picnic basket was loaded and ready for Chase to carry to his rental car.

" 'Morning," she greeted him.

" 'Morning," Chase returned, leaning forward to kiss her.

The kiss seemed instinctive on both their parts. A kiss, Lesley noticed, that was exchanged without doubt or hesitation.

Suddenly their smiles faded and her lungs emptied of air. It wasn't supposed to happen like this. She was inches, seconds, from walking into his arms before she caught herself.

Chase, however, felt no such restraint and reached for her, pulling her toward him. Even with her mind crying no, she waited impatiently for his mouth to touch hers.

His lips were gentle, as if he were aware of her feelings.

"I love it when you do that," he whispered, kissing her neck.

"Do what?" she asked, sighing deeply.

He groaned. "You just did it again. That sigh. It tells me so much more than you'd ever be willing to say."

"Don't be ridiculous." She tried to ease away from him, but felt his breath warm and moist against her throat — and couldn't move. His fingers loosened the top button of her blouse.

"I . . . I don't think this is a good idea," Lesley murmured as he backed her against the door. He braced his hands on either side of her head, his eyes gazing into hers.

"I don't want you to *think*. I want

you to feel." He kissed her then with the same wicked sweetness that had broken her resolve seconds before. She sighed, the same sigh he'd mentioned earlier, and regretted it immediately.

"Lesley, I don't know what to do." He leaned his forehead against hers.

"Kiss me again." She held his face with her hands, buried her fingers in the thickness of his hair and directed his lips back to hers. By the time they drew apart, both were panting and breathless.

For a moment neither of them said anything. "I think you might be right," he finally said with reluctance. "This isn't such a good idea, after all. One taste of you would never be enough. I'm greedy, Lesley. I want it all. It's better not to start what we can't finish."

He reached for the picnic basket and took it outside. Lesley felt weak and shaken. She wouldn't have believed it possible for any man to evoke such an intense reaction with a few kisses.

Her knees were trembling as she grabbed her knapsack and purse and followed him out the door. Chase stored her things beside the picnic basket in the trunk. He helped her into the passenger seat and got into the car a moment later, waiting until she'd adjusted her seat belt before he started the engine.

Neither of them had much to say on the long drive to Paradise. Lesley had planned to play the role of tour guide as she had previously, pointing out interesting facts along the way, but changed her mind. She was going to mention that Mount Rainier National Park was one of the first parks ever established — in 1899. But it wasn't important to tell him that, not if it meant disturbing the peaceful silence they shared.

Lesley loved Mount Rainier and the way it stood guard over the Pacific Northwest. The view of the mountain from Seattle was often breathtaking. Her appreciation increased even more when she saw the look in Chase's eyes as they drove the twisting road through the forest-thick area. He surprised her with his knowledge of trees.

"Everyone recognizes a Douglas fir when they see one, don't they?" he teased.

"No."

They stopped at a campsite and took a break. When Lesley returned from using the facilities, she saw Chase wandering through the mossy, fern-draped valley. She joined him, feeling a sense of closeness and solemnity with Chase, as though they were standing on holy ground. The trees surrounding them were tall and massive, the forest a lush green. Breathing deeply, Lesley felt the fullness of beauty standing there with him. The air was sharp, clean, vibrant with the scent of evergreens.

Chase took her hand and entwined his fingers with hers. "Are you ready?" he asked.

Lesley nodded, uncertain what she was agreeing to, and for once in her life not caring.

They got back in the car and in companionable silence traveled the rest of the way to Paradise. Since they hadn't eaten breakfast, Chase suggested they have their picnic, which they did. He finished the chocolate chip cookies she'd brought for him, praising them lavishly.

Afterward, Lesley put on her boots and they walked the trails through the open, subalpine meadowlands, which were shedding their cold blankets of snow.

"You know what I love most here? The flowers, their color, the way they fight through the cold and stand proudly against the hillside as if to say they've accomplished something important," Lesley said as they climbed up the steep path.

"The flowers respond the way most

of us do, don't you think?" Chase asked.

"How's that?"

"They respond to *life.* To the power and force of life. I feel it here and you do, too. It's like standing on a boulder and looking out over the world and saying, 'Here I am. I've done it.' "

"And what exactly *have* you done, Chase Goodman?"

He chuckled. "I haven't figured it out yet, but this feeling is too good to waste."

She laughed. "I know what you mean."

They hiked for a couple of hours, and ascended as far as the tree line. The beauty of the hills and valleys was unending, spilling out before them like an Impressionist painting, in vibrant hues of purple, rose and white.

After their hike, they explored the visitor center, then headed back to the car.

Lesley was exhausted. The day had been full and exciting. Over the years, she'd visited Paradise countless times and had always enjoyed herself, but not the way she had today with Chase. With him, she'd experienced a spiritual wonder, a feeling of joy, a new connection with nature. She couldn't think of a logical way to explain it any more than she could say why his kisses affected her so strongly.

When they arrived back in Seattle, Eric and Kevin, Daisy's two boys, ran out to the car to greet them.

"Hi, Lesley," Eric, the oldest boy,

said, eyeing Chase.

"Hello, boys. This is Chase."

Chase cordially shook hands with the youngsters. "Howdy, boys."

"You're sure big. Even bigger 'n Lesley."

Lesley wasn't sure if that was a compliment or not.

"We came to see if you had any cookies left."

"Mom said you might have some more," Kevin chimed in.

"Yup, I saved some for you."

"But don't forget she made them for me," Chase said. "You boys should make sure I'm willing to share the loot before you ask Lesley."

"She used to make them for us. So we've got dibs."

"You gonna share or not?" Kevin asked, hands on his hips, implying a showdown if necessary.

Chase rubbed the side of his jaw as if giving the matter consideration.

"Those boys bothering you?" Daisy shouted from the front door.

"We just want our share of Lesley's cookies before Chase eats 'em all."

"I'll buy you cookies," Daisy promised, throwing an apologetic look at Lesley. For her part, Lesley was enjoying this exchange, especially the way Chase interacted with the two boys. Tony had treated Daisy's sons as pests and shooed them away whenever they came around. Although he worked with children, he had little rapport with them outside the classroom.

"We don't want any *store-bought* cookies," Eric argued.

"Don't try and bake any, either,

Mom, not after last time." He looked at Lesley, and whispered, "Even my friend's dog wouldn't eat them."

Lesley smothered a giggle.

"Will you or won't you give us some cookies?" Eric demanded of Chase.

Chase himself was having trouble not smiling. "I guess I don't have much choice. You two have a prior claim and any judge in the land would take that into account."

"Does that mean he will or he won't?" Kevin asked his brother.

"He will," Eric answered. "I think."

"But only if you help us unload the car," Chase said, giving them both a few things to haul inside.

Lesley emptied the cookie jar, setting aside a handful for Chase, and doled out the boys' well-earned reward. While Chase was dealing with the picnic basket, she absently checked her answering machine.

"Lesley, it's Tony. I've been doing a lot of thinking lately and thought we should get together to talk. April's out of town this week visiting her mother, so give me a call as soon as you can."

Lesley felt as if someone had just hit her. Instinctively her hands went to her stomach, and she stood frozen in a desperate effort to catch her breath.

She turned slowly around, not knowing what to do, and discovered Chase standing there, staring at her.

FIVE

"Well," Chase said, studying Lesley closely. "Are you going to call him?"

"No."

"You're sure?"

He seemed to doubt Lesley and that upset her, possibly because she *wasn't* sure. Part of her wanted to speak to Tony. School had been out for more than a week now and she was starved for the sight of him. Admitting her weakness, even to herself, demanded rigorous, painful honesty. Tony was married, and it sickened her that she felt this way.

"I'm sure," she snapped, then added, "although it's none of your business."

He nodded, his eyes guarded as though he wanted to believe her but wasn't convinced he should. "Are you going to invite me in for a cup of coffee?"

Lesley stared at him, not knowing what to say. She needed privacy in order to analyze her feelings, but at the same time, she didn't want Chase to leave, because once he did, she'd be forced to confront her weakness for Tony.

Eric came into the kitchen, munching loudly on a cookie. "Lesley's the best cook I ever met," he announced, looking proud to be her neighbor. His jeans had large rips in the knees and his T-shirt was badly stained, but his cheerful expression was infectious.

"A better cook than Mom," Kevin agreed, rubbing his forearm over his mouth to remove any crumbs.

"Even Dr. Seuss is a better cook than Mom. Remember the time she made us green eggs and ham for breakfast? Except they weren't supposed to be." Both boys laughed and grabbed another cookie.

"Say, you two ever been fishing?" Chase asked unexpectedly.

"Nope." They gazed up at Chase with wide, eager eyes.

"I was planning to ask Lesley to go fishing tomorrow and I thought it might be fun if you two came along. You think you could talk your mom into letting you join us?"

"I'll ask," Eric said, racing from the

kitchen.

"I want to ask," Kevin shouted, running after his brother.

Lesley made a pot of coffee. She wasn't gullible; she knew exactly why Chase had included the boys. He wanted to see her again and knew she wouldn't refuse him if it meant disappointing her ragamuffin neighbors. She said as much when she brought two mugs of coffee to the table.

"What would you do if I said I couldn't go with you?" she asked, sitting across from him.

The healing calm she'd experienced earlier with Chase on Mount Rainier had been shattered by Tony's call. She hadn't realized how frail that newfound peace had been or how easily it could be destroyed. She hated the fact that Tony continued to wield such power over her, especially when she felt she'd made strides in letting go of her love for him.

"The boys and I'd miss you," Chase said after a moment, "but I'd never disappoint those two. Every boy should go fishing at some point in his life. I'd like it if you'd come, but I'll understand if you'd prefer to stay home." He sipped his coffee and seemed to be waiting for a response from her.

"Would it be all right if I let you know in the morning?"

"Of course."

The front door flew open and Eric and Kevin shot into the room like bullets, breathless with excitement. "Mom said we could go! But she needs to know how much money we need and what we should bring."

"Tell her you don't need a dime and all you have to bring is an extra set of clothes."

"What time?"

"Six sounds good."

"In the *morning?*" Kevin's eyes rounded with dismay. "We don't usually get up before nine."

"You want to catch trout, don't you?"

"Sure, but . . ."

"We'll be ready," Eric said, elbowing his brother in the ribs. "Isn't that right, Kevin?"

"Ow. Yeah, we'll be ready."

"Good. Then I'll see you boys bright and early tomorrow morning." Chase ushered them to the door, while Lesley sat at the table, hiding her amusement.

When Chase returned, he surprised

her by taking one last sip of his coffee and carrying the mug to her sink. He came back to the table, placed his hand on her shoulder and kissed her cheek. "I'll talk to you later."

"You're leaving?" Suddenly it became vital that he stay because once he left, she feared the temptation to return Tony's call would be too strong to control, too easy to rationalize. Standing abruptly, she folded her arms and stared up at him, struggling with herself.

"You don't want me to go?"

She shrugged and finally admitted the truth. "I . . . want you to help me understand why Tony would phone me out of the blue like this. I want you to help me figure out what I should do, but more importantly, I need you to remind me how wrong it

would be to call him. I can't — won't
— betray my own principles."

"Sorry," Chase said, sounding
genuinely regretful. "Those are things
you've got to figure out on your
own."

"But . . ."

"I'll give you a call in the morning."

"Aren't you going to kiss me?"

He hesitated and desire was clear
on his face. "I'd like nothing better,
but I don't think I should."

"Why not?" She moved closer, so
close she could feel his breath against
her face, so close that all she needed
to do was ease forward and her lips
would meet his.

"I don't think it'd be a good idea
just now." His voice was low.

"I *need* you to kiss me," she said,
pressing her palms against his shirt

and waiting.

"I wish . . ." she continued.

His breathing was erratic, but so was her own.

"What do you wish?" His mouth wandered to her neck and she sighed at the feel of his lips against her skin. She angled her head back, revealing her eagerness for his touch.

"You already know what I want," she whispered.

He planted slow kisses on her throat, pausing to moisten the hollow with the tip of his tongue. Shivers of awareness rippled down her arms.

Her mouth sought his and he kissed her, his lips soft and undemanding. She slipped her arms around his neck and nestled into his arms, needing the security of his touch to ground her in reality.

When he kissed her again, she moaned, lifting her hand to the back of his head, urging him closer. "Oh, Chase," she breathed once the kiss had ended.

He raised his head and touched her forehead with his lips. "A man could get used to hearing a woman say his name like that."

"Oh." Her response sounded inane, but conversation was beyond her.

"Marry me, Lesley."

She risked a glance at his face and felt emotion well up in her throat. Blinking rapidly, she managed to hold the tears at bay.

"All right," he said. "We'll do this your way, in increments. Will you join the boys and me in the morning?"

Lesley nodded.

"I was hoping you would." He

kissed the tip of her nose. "I have to leave now. Trust me, I'd much rather stay, but I can't and we both know why."

Lesley did know.

It wasn't fair to use Chase as a shield against Tony. She would have to stand alone, make her own decisions, and Chase understood that more clearly than she had herself.

"I'll see you at six in the morning," he whispered, and released her. As if he couldn't wait that long to kiss her again, he lowered his mouth to hers, kissed her longingly, then slowly turned away.

The sound of the front door closing followed seconds later, and Lesley stood in the middle of her kitchen with the phone just inches away.

■ ■ ■ ■

"A trout can sure put up a big fight," Eric said with a satisfied look in his brother's direction after he'd caught his first fish.

The four of them were standing on the banks of Green River, their lines dangling in the water. Through pure luck, Eric had managed to catch the first trout. While Chase helped the boy remove the squirming fish from the line and rebait his hook, Lesley whispered reassurances to Kevin.

"Don't worry, you'll snag one, too."

"But what if I don't?" Kevin asked, hanging his head. "Eric *always* gets everything first just 'cause he's older. It isn't fair. It just isn't fair."

No sooner were the words out of his mouth than his line dipped with such force that he nearly lost his fishing rod. His triumphant gaze flew to Lesley. "I've got one!"

Chase immediately went over to the younger boy, coaxing him as he had Eric, tutoring him until the boy had reeled in the trout and Chase was able to take the good-size fish from the hook.

"Is mine bigger than Eric's?" Kevin demanded.

"You'll have to check that for yourself."

"Yup, mine's bigger," Kevin announced a moment later with a smug look.

Lesley found the younger boy's conviction amusing, but said nothing. To prove his point, Kevin held up both fish and asked Lesley to judge, but it was impossible to tell.

They spent most of the morning fishing, until both boys had reached their limit. Although Chase had brought Lesley a fishing rod, she didn't do much fishing herself. Twice she got a fish on the line, but both times she let the boys reel them in for her. Chase did the same, letting the boys experience the thrill.

By eleven o'clock, all four were famished.

"Let's have trout for lunch," Chase suggested.

"I thought Lesley made sandwiches," Kevin said, eyeing the fish suspiciously. "I don't like fish, unless it's fish and chips, and then I'll eat it."

"That's because you've never had anyone cook trout the way the Indians do." Chase explained a method of slow cooking, wrapping the fish in leaves and mud and burying them in the coals, which had even Lesley's mouth watering in anticipation. He also explained the importance of never allowing the fish they'd caught to go to waste. The boys nodded solemnly as if they understood the wisdom of his words. By then, Lesley guessed, they both thought Chase walked on water.

"I'm going to need your help," he said, instructing the boys to gather kindling for the fire. "Then you can help me clean the trout."

"You won't need me for this, will you?" Lesley asked hopefully.

"Women are afraid of guts," Eric explained for Chase's benefit.

"Is that so?"

"They go all weird over that kind of

stuff. Mom's the same way. One time, the neighbor's cat, a black one named Midnight . . . you know Midnight, don't you, Lesley?"

She nodded.

"Midnight brought a dead bird into the yard and Mom started going all weird and yelling. We thought someone was trying to murder her."

"I thought Dad was back," Eric inserted, and Chase's eyes connected briefly with Lesley's and for an instant fire leapt into his eyes.

"Anyway, Mom asked Kevin and me to bury it. I don't think she's ever forgiven Midnight, either. She gives him mean looks whenever he comes to visit and shoos him away."

While the boys were discussing a woman's aversion to the sight of blood, Lesley brought out the plastic tablecloth and spread it over a picnic table close to where they'd parked the car.

"That's another thing," Eric said knowingly, motioning toward her. "A woman wants to make everything fancy. Real men don't eat on a tablecloth. Kevin and I never would if it wasn't for Mom and Lesley."

"Don't forget Grandma," Kevin said.

"Right, and Grandma, too."

"Those feminine touches can be nice, though," Chase told the boys. "I live in a big log cabin up in Alaska and it gets mighty lonesome during the winters. Last January I would've done just about anything to have a pretty face smiling at me across the dinner table, even if it meant having to eat on a tablecloth. I wouldn't have cared if she'd spread out ten of them. It would've been a small price to pay for her company."

"You mean you *wanted* a woman with you?" Eric sounded surprised.

"Men like having women around?" Kevin asked.

"Of course," Chase returned casually.

"My dad doesn't feel like that. He said he was glad to be rid of us. He said lots of mean things that made Mom cry and he hit her sometimes, too."

Chase crouched down in front of Eric and Kevin and talked to them for several minutes. She couldn't hear everything he said, because she was making trips back and forth to the car, but she knew whatever it was had an impact on the boys. She was touched when the three of them hugged.

After a while, the fire Chase had built had burned down to hot coals. The boys and Chase wrapped the cleaned fish in a bed of leaves and packed them in mud before burying them in the dirt, which they covered with the hot coals.

"While we're waiting," Chase suggested, "we'll try those sandwiches Lesley packed and go exploring."

"Great." After collecting their sandwiches, both boys eagerly accompanied Chase on a nearby trail. Lesley chose to stay behind. Trekking into the woods, chasing after those two, was beyond her. She got a lounge chair she'd packed, opened it and gratefully sank down on it.

She must have dozed off because

she woke with both boys staring down at her, studying her as if she were a specimen under a microscope.

"She's awake," Eric cried.

"Let's eat," Kevin said. "I'm starved."

Lesley had the plastic plates and plastic silverware set out on the table, along with a large bag of potato chips, veggies and a cake she'd baked the night before.

Chase dug up the fish, scraped away the dried mud and peeled back the leaves. The tantalizing aroma of the trout took Lesley by surprise. Until then she hadn't thought she was hungry.

They ate until they were stuffed, until they couldn't force down another morsel. Chase and the boys conscientiously packed up the garbage and loaded the vehicle after Lesley had wrapped the leftovers — not that there were many.

Eric and Kevin fell asleep in the backseat on the ride home.

"They really enjoyed themselves," Lesley whispered. "They'll remember this day all their lives. It was very sweet of you to invite them along."

She watched as his gaze briefly moved to his rearview mirror and he glanced at the boys. "I'd like to meet their father in a dark alley someday. I have no tolerance for a man who hits a woman."

"He has a drinking problem," Lesley said.

"Is that an excuse?"

"No, just an explanation."

"The man should be punished for telling his sons he's glad to be rid of them. What kind of father would say such a thing?"

He didn't seem to expect an answer, which was just as well since Lesley didn't have one.

Daisy was back from her computer classes by the time they arrived at the house. The boys woke up when Chase cut the engine. As soon as they realized they were home, they darted out of the car and into the house, talking excitedly about their adventures.

Daisy came out of the house with her sons and ordered them to help unload the car for Lesley, which they did willingly.

Lesley had been neighbors and friends with Daisy for three years. She'd watched this no-nonsense woman make some hard decisions in that time, but never once had she seen her friend cry. There were tears in Daisy's eyes now.

"Thank you," she said to Chase in a tremulous voice.

"No problem. I was happy to have them with us. You're raising two fine boys there, Daisy. You should be proud of them."

"Oh, darn." She held an index finger under each eye. "You're going to have me bawling here in a minute. I just wanted to thank you both."

"Daisy?" Lesley asked gently. "Is everything all right?"

"Of course everything's all right. A woman can shed a few tears now and then, can't she?"

"Sure, but . . ."

"I know. I'm making a fool of myself. It's just that I appreciate what you did for my boys. I've never seen them so excited and so happy." Lesley wasn't expecting to be hugged, but Daisy reached for her, nearly squeezing the breath from her lungs. "I want to thank you for being my friend," she murmured, wiping her hand under her nose. Then she returned to her house.

Eric and Kevin were off, eager to relate their escapades to their neighborhood friends.

Chase followed Lesley into the kitchen. He helped her unload the picnic basket, then stopped abruptly, looking over at her.

"Is something the matter?" she asked.

"It looks like you've got a message on your answering machine."

Lesley's heart felt frozen in her

chest. Trying to be nonchalant about it, she walked over and pushed the playback button. This time, Tony's voice didn't rip through her like the blade of a knife. In fact, hearing him again so soon felt anticlimactic.

"Lesley, it's Tony. When you didn't return my call, I stopped by the house. You weren't home. I need to talk to you. Call me soon. Please."

Lesley looked at Chase, wishing she could read his thoughts, wishing she could gauge her own. His eyes were darker than she'd ever seen them and his jaw was stiff.

"Are you going to contact him?"

She wasn't any more confident than she'd been earlier. "I don't know."

"I see."

"You want to remind me he's a married man, don't you?" she cried.

"I know that, Chase. I have no idea why he's calling or what he wants from me."

"Get real, Lesley. You know exactly what he wants. Didn't he say April's out of town?"

"Tony's not like that." Again, she didn't understand why she felt the need to defend him. She'd done it so often that it came naturally to her, she supposed. Although, she did have to wonder if Tony might be unfaithful to April, as he'd been to her.

"You know him better than I do," Chase admitted grudgingly. "I've got to get back," he said, as though he couldn't get away from her fast enough.

"Are you interviewing more . . . applicants?" she asked him on the way to the door, making conversation, not wanting their day to end on a sour note.

"Yes," he said briskly. "Several."

His answer surprised her. "When?"

"I talked to some last night and I have more scheduled for later this afternoon and evening."

"You'll call me?" she asked, trailing after him.

He hesitated, not looking at her. An eternity seemed to pass before he nodded. "All right," he said curtly.

Lesley longed to reassure him; that was what Chase was waiting for her to do. To promise him she wouldn't call Tony. But she couldn't tell him that. She hadn't decided yet. She remembered what he'd said about not wanting to compete with another man for a woman's affections. What Chase didn't understand was that she'd never try to play one man against another.

"I'll look forward to hearing from you," she said. To her own ears she sounded oddly formal. She stood on the other side of the screen door, watching him walk away from her. She had the craziest feeling that he was taking a piece of her heart with him.

She waited until his car was gone before she breathed again. She told herself she couldn't possibly know a man for such a short while and adequately judge her feelings. She was attracted to him, but any other woman with two eyes in her head would be, too.

Then there was Tony. She'd loved him for so long she didn't know how to stop. He'd been an integral part of her life and without him her world felt empty and meaningless.

Lesley walked back into her kitchen and listened to the message again. She thought about phoning Lori and asking for advice, but decided against it. Lori had said she'd get back to her later, and she hadn't yet.

Daisy was the more logical choice, although her feelings about Tony were well-known. Lesley found her neighbor in the backyard, wearing a bikini, soaking up the sun on a chaise longue while propping an aluminum shield under her chin. Amused, Lesley stood by the fence and studied her.

"Where in heaven's name did you get *that?*" Lesley asked.

"Don't get excited. It's one of those microwave pizza boxes the boys like, with those silver linings. I figured I'd put it to good use now that they're finished with the pizza."

"Honestly, Daisy, you crack me up."

"I've only got so much time to get any sun. I've got to make the most of it."

"I know, I know."

"Where'd Chase take off to?"

Lesley looked away. "He had to get back to his hotel. Did I tell you eight hundred women responded to his billboard?"

Daisy's eyes were closed. "Seems to me it's a shame you're not one of them. What's the matter, Lesley, is it beneath your dignity?"

"Yes," she snapped.

Daisy's sigh revealed how exasperated she was with Lesley. "That's too bad, sweetie, because that man's worth ten Tonys."

Lesley's fingers closed around the top of the fence. "It's funny that you should mention Tony because he's been calling me."

"What does that poor excuse of a man have to say for himself?"

"He claims he needs to talk to me."

"I'll just bet."

"He left two messages and Chase was here both times when I listened to them."

Daisy shook her head. "Chase isn't the type to stand still for that nonsense. Did he set you straight?"

"Daisy! I don't need a man to tell me what to do and I resent you even suggesting such a thing." She remembered, a little guiltily, that she *had* asked Chase to help her sort out her feelings for Tony as well as her moral obligations.

"You're right, of course. Neither of us truly needs a man for *anything*. I don't and you've proved you don't, either. But you know, having one around can be a real comfort at times."

"I don't know what to do," Lesley said, worrying her lower lip.

"About Chase and all those women?"

She was astonished by the way Daisy always brought the conversation back to Chase. "No! About Tony calling me."

"You've been miserable because that slimeball dumped you," Daisy went on with barely a pause. "I find it ironic that when you meet up with a really decent guy, Tony comes sniffin' around. Does this guy have radar or what?"

Lesley smiled. "I doubt it."

"He couldn't tolerate the thought of you with another man, you know."

"Don't be ridiculous! He didn't want me, Daisy. You seem to be forgetting that."

"Of course he wants you. For Tony it's a matter of pride to keep two women in love with him. Don't kid yourself. His ego eats it up."

"He's married."

Daisy snorted. "When has that ever stopped a man?"

"I'm sure you're wrong." Here she was defending him *again* although she didn't even know what he wanted from her.

"Listen, sweetie, you might have a college degree, but when it comes to men, you're as naive as those kids you teach. Why do you think Tony didn't want you transferring to another school? He wants to keep his eye on you. Trust me, the minute you show any interest in another man, he'll be there like stink on —"

"I get the picture, Daisy."

"Fine, but do you get the message?"

Lesley gnawed at her lip. "I think so."

Daisy lowered the aluminum shield. She turned her head to look at Lesley. "You're afraid, aren't you? Afraid of what'll happen if you call Tony back."

Lesley nodded.

"Are you still in love with that jerk?"

Once more she nodded.

"Oh, Lesley, you idiot. You don't need him, not when you've got someone like Chase. He's crazy about you, but he isn't stupid. He's not going to ram his head against a brick wall, and who could blame him? Not me."

"I hardly know Chase."

"What more do you *need* to know?"

"Daisy, he's looking for a wife."

"So what?" Her neighbor asked impatiently.

"I'm not in love with Chase."

"Do you like him?"

"Of course I do. Otherwise I wouldn't continue to see him."

"What are you expecting, sweetie? This guy is manna from heaven. If you want to spend the rest of your life mooning over Tony, feel free. As far as I'm concerned, that guy's going to do his best to make you miserable for as long as he can."

"Chase is from Alaska," Lesley argued.

"So? You don't have any family

here. There's nothing holding you back other than Tony, is there? Is a married man worth all that grief, Lesley?"

"No." How small her voice sounded, how uncertain.

"Do you want to lose Chase?"

"I don't know . . ."

"You don't *know?* Sometimes I want to clobber you, Lesley. Where do you think you'd ever find another man as good as Chase? But if that doesn't concern you, then far be it from me to point out the obvious." She swung her legs from the chaise longue. "If you want my advice, I'd say go for it and marry the guy. I doubt that you'll be sorry."

Lesley wished she could be as sure of that, but she wasn't. She wasn't even sure how she was going to get

through another night without calling Tony.

Six

Chase forced himself to relax. He wasn't being fair to the women he'd interviewed. He tried, heaven knew he'd tried, to concentrate on what they'd said, but it hadn't worked, not in a single case. And this had been going on for several days.

He'd ask a question, listen intently for the first minute or two, and then his mind would drift. What irritated him most was the subject that dominated his thoughts so completely.

Lesley.

She was in love with Tony, although

she was struggling to hide it. Not from him, but from herself. All the signs were there.

If he had more time, he might have a chance with Lesley. But he didn't. Even if he could afford a couple of months to court her, it might not be enough.

The best thing, the only thing, he could do was accept that whatever they'd so briefly had was over, cut his losses and do what he could to make up for wasted time.

"That's the last of them for this evening," Sandra said, letting herself into the room. The door clicked softly behind her.

"Good." He was exhausted to the bone.

"I've got appointments starting first thing tomorrow morning. Are you sure you're up to this?"

He nodded, although he wasn't sure of anything. He could hardly keep the faces and the stories straight.

Sandra hesitated. "Has anyone caught your fancy yet?"

Chase chuckled, not because he found her question amusing, but because he was susceptible to one of the most basic human flaws — wanting what he couldn't have. He wanted Lesley. "The woman I'd like to marry is in love with someone else and won't marry me."

"Isn't that the way it generally works?" Sandra offered sympathetically.

"It must," he said, stretching out his legs and crossing them at the ankles. He wasn't accustomed to so much sitting and was getting restless.

The city was beginning to wear on him, too, and the thought of his cabin on the tundra became more appealing by the minute.

"Is there one woman who's stuck out in your mind?" He motioned for Sandra to sit down and she did, taking the chair across from him.

"A couple," she said. "Do you remember Anna Lincoln and LaDonna Ransom?"

Chase didn't, not immediately. "Describe them to me."

"LaDonna's that petite blonde you saw yesterday evening, the one who's working in the King County Assessor's office."

Try as he might, Chase couldn't recall the woman, not when there'd been so many. There'd been several blondes, and countless faces and little

that made one stand out over another.

"But I hesitate to recommend her. She's a fragile little thing, and I don't know how well she'd adjust to winters that far north. Seattle's climate is temperate and nothing like what you experience. But . . . she was sweet, and I think you'd grow to love her, given the opportunity."

"What about Anna Lincoln?"

"We chatted for a bit before the interview and she seemed to be a nice girl. Ambitious, too. Of course there was the one drawback." Sandra shrugged. "She's not very pretty, at least not when you compare her to a lot of the other women who've ap-plied."

"Beauty doesn't count for much as far as I'm concerned. I'm not exactly a movie star myself, you know."

Sandra must have felt obliged to argue with him because she made something of a fuss, contradicting him. By the time she'd finished, she had him sounding like he should consider running for Mr. Universe.

"At any rate, I liked Anna and I think she'd suit you. If you want I'll get her file."

"Please."

Sandra left and returned a couple of minutes later with the file. Chase was reading it over when she said good-night. He waved absently as he scanned the application and his few notes. There wasn't a picture enclosed, which might have jogged his memory. The details she'd written down about herself described at least twenty other women he'd interviewed in the past few days.

He set the file aside and relaxed, leaning back in his chair, wondering if Anna's lips were as soft and pliable as Lesley's, or if she fit in his arms as though she'd been made for him. Probably not. No use trying to fool himself.

He reread the information and, exhaling sharply with defeat, set aside the file. At the rate things were going, he'd return to Twin Creeks without the bride he'd come to find.

"Lori?" Lesley was so excited to find her friend at home that her voice rose unnaturally high.

"Lesley? Hi."

"Hi, yourself. I've been waiting to hear from you. We were going to get together this week, remember?"

"We were? Oh, right, I did say I'd call you, didn't I? I'm sorry, I haven't had a chance. Oh, Les, you'll never guess what happened. Larry asked me to marry him!" She let out a scream that sounded as though she were being strangled.

"Lori!"

"I know, I've got to stop doing that, but every time I think of Larry and me together, I get so excited I can hardly stand it."

"You haven't been dating him that long, have you?"

"Long enough. I'm crazy about this guy, Lesley, and for once in my life I've found a man who feels the same way about me."

"Congratulations!" Lesley put as much punch into the word as she could. She *was* thrilled for Lori, and wished her fellow teacher and Larry every happiness. But in the same breath, in the same heartbeat, she was so jealous she wanted to weep.

Truth demanded a price and being honest with herself had taken its toll on Lesley all week. First, she'd been forced to admit she still loved Tony, despite all her efforts to put him out of her life. It was hopeless, useless and masochistic. She didn't need Daisy to tell her she was setting herself up for heartache. Not when she could see it herself.

Despite the temptation, she hadn't returned Tony's calls. However, it wasn't her sense of honor that had prompted her forbearance, nor had it been her sense of right and wrong.

Good old-fashioned fear was what kept her away from the phone. Fear of what she might do if Tony admitted he'd made a mistake and wanted her back in his life. Fear of what she might become if he came to her, claiming he loved her, needed her.

On the heels of this painful insight came the news of Lori's engagement. Now she and Jo Ann were the only two single women left at the school. And Jo Ann didn't count, not technically.

Jo Ann had separated from her husband a year earlier and she'd taken back her maiden name. But recently they'd been talking. It wouldn't surprise Lesley if the two of them decided to make another go of their marriage.

Now Lori was engaged.

"Larry wants a short engagement, which is fine with me," she was saying. "I'd like it if we could have the wedding before school starts this fall, and he's agreed. You'll be one of my bridesmaids, won't you?"

"I'd be honored." That would make six times now that Lesley had stood up for friends. What was that old saying? Always a bridesmaid, never a bride. It certainly applied in her case.

In the fall she'd be returning to the same school, the same classroom, the one directly down from Tony's. April's class was on the other side of the building. They'd all return, enthusiastic about the new school year, eager to get started after the long break.

Tony would glance at her with that special look in his eyes and she wouldn't be able to glance away. He'd know in a heartbeat that she still loved him, and worse, so would April and everyone else on staff. That humiliation far outweighed the likelihood of being the only unmarried faculty member.

Lesley knew she never should've let Tony talk her out of transferring to another school. Perhaps she'd asked for another assignment just so he'd beg her to stay; she didn't know anymore, didn't trust herself or her motives.

"Larry talked to my dad and formally asked for my hand in marriage," Lori was saying when Lesley pulled her thoughts back to her friend. "He's so traditional and sweet. It's funny, Les, but when it's right, it's right, and you know it in your gut. It wouldn't have mattered if we'd dated three months or three years."

"Hadn't you met Larry a while ago?"

"Yeah. Apparently. He's a friend of my brother's, but I don't *remember* meeting him until this spring, although he claims I did. He pretends to be insulted that I've forgotten."

Lesley smiled. Lori's happiness sang through the wire like a melodious love song, full of spirit and joy. They spoke for a few minutes longer, of getting together with three of Lori's other friends and choosing the dresses, but it was all rather vague.

Jealous. That was how Lesley felt. Jealous of one of her best friends. She hated admitting it, but there was no other way to explain the hard knot in her stomach. It wasn't that she wished Lori and Larry anything but the best.

But her feelings were wrapped around memories of the past, of standing alone, helpless and lost. Abandoned.

When she finished talking to Lori, Lesley called a florist friend and had a congratulatory bouquet sent to Lori and Larry with her warmest wishes.

Housework, Lesley decided. That was what a woman did when she suffered from guilt. It was either that or bury herself in a gallon of gourmet ice cream. She stripped her bed, stuffed the sheets in the washer and was hanging them on the line when Eric and Kevin found her.

"Is Chase coming over today?" Eric wanted to know.

"He didn't say," she answered as noncommittally as she could. She didn't want to disappoint them, or encourage them, either.

"Can you call him and ask?"

Lesley shoved a clothespin onto a sheet, anchoring it. "I don't have his phone number," she said, realizing it for the first time.

"He'll be calling you, won't he?"

"I . . . don't know." She'd asked him to and he'd said he would, but that wasn't any guarantee. He'd been annoyed with her when they parted, convinced she'd contact Tony despite her shaky reassurance otherwise.

Chase was an intelligent and sensitive man; he knew better than to involve himself in a dead-end relationship. It wouldn't surprise her if he never contacted her again.

The thought struck her hard and fast. The pain it produced shocked her. She hadn't realized how much she'd come to treasure their brief time together.

"What do you *mean* you don't know if he'll call you again?" Eric demanded. "You *have* to see him again because Kevin and me wrote him a letter to thank him for taking us fishing."

"Mom made us," Kevin volunteered. His front tooth was missing and Lesley noticed its absence for the first time.

She caught the younger boy by the chin and angled his head toward the light, although he squirmed. "Kevin, you lost your tooth. When did this happen?"

"Last night."

"Congratulations," she said, releasing him. "Did you leave it out for the Tooth Fairy?"

The boy rolled his eyes. "I don't believe in that silly stuff anymore and neither does Eric."

"What do you expect when they've got me for a mother?" Daisy said, stepping out the back porch, her hands on her hips. "I never did believe in feeding kids all that garbage about Santa Claus and the Easter bunny. Life's hard enough without their own mother filling their heads with that kind of nonsense."

"We get gifts and candy and other stuff," Kevin felt obliged to inform Lesley, "but we know who gave them to us. Mom gave me a dollar for the tooth."

"He already spent it, too, on gum and candy."

"I shared, didn't I?"

"Boys, why don't you run along,"

Daisy said.

"What about the letter?"

"Give it to Lesley and let her worry about it." With that, her neighbor returned to the house.

What Lesley had told the boys about not knowing Chase's phone number was a half-truth. There was always the number on the billboard. If she hadn't heard from him by that evening, she'd leave a message for him through the answering service, although she doubted it would ever reach him.

After a polite knock, Sandra let herself into Chase's makeshift office in the suite he'd rented. He'd interviewed ten more women that morning and was scheduled to meet another fifteen that afternoon and evening.

He hadn't talked to or seen Lesley in two days and the temptation to call her or even drive over to see her was gaining momentum. He was trying, really trying, to meet a woman he liked as much as Lesley. Thus far he hadn't succeeded. Hadn't come anywhere *close* to succeeding.

"Does the name Lesley Campbell mean anything to you?" Sandra asked unexpectedly.

Chase straightened as a chill shot through him. "Yes, why?"

"She left a message with the answering service. Apparently she explained that she wasn't responding to your billboard ad. She wanted it understood that the two of you know each other."

"She left a message?"

219

"Yes." Sandra handed him the pink slip. "I thought it might be a trick. Some of the applicants have tried various methods to get your attention."

Chase didn't need to be reminded of that. Flowers arrived almost daily, along with elaborately wrapped presents. A few of the gifts had shocked him. He hadn't accepted any of them. The floral bouquets he had delivered to a nearby nursing home and the gifts were dispensed with quickly. He left their disposal in Sandra's capable hands.

One woman, a day earlier, had shown up in full winter garb, carrying a long-barreled shotgun as though that would prove she was ready, willing and able to withstand the harsh winters of the Arctic. He wasn't sure what the gun was meant to signify.

Chase supposed she'd rented the outfit from a costume store. She resembled Daniel Boone more than she did a prospective wife. Chase had lost patience with her and sent her on her way.

He glanced down at the message slip in his hand and tried to decide what to do. Returning Lesley's call could just prolong the inevitable. He wondered if she'd spoken to Tony and what had come of their conversation. The minute he learned she had, it would be over for them. Possibly it was already over.

Objectivity was beyond him at this point. As far as he was concerned, Tony was bad news. All the man represented for Lesley was heartache and grief. If she wasn't smart enough to figure that out for herself, then he couldn't help her.

He waited until Sandra had left the room before he called Lesley. She answered on the second ring. The sound of her voice produced an empty, achy feeling that surprised him; he'd been unaware she had such power to hurt him. He had no one to blame but himself. If Lesley hurt him, it was because *he'd* allowed it.

"It's Chase."

"Chase . . ." she said breathlessly. "Thank you for returning my call. I wasn't sure you'd get my message."

"How are you?" He'd never been a brilliant conversationalist, but he was generally more adept than this.

"Fine. How about you?"

"Busy."

"Yeah, me, too."

Silence. Chase didn't know if he should break it by saying something or wait for her to do it. They hadn't fought, hadn't spoken so much as a cross word to each other. He couldn't even say they'd disagreed, but there was a gap between them that had appeared after Tony's first call and widened with the second one.

"Eric and Kevin were asking about you," Lesley said before the silence threatened to go on forever. "I didn't know what to tell them."

"I see."

"They wrote you a letter and asked me to give it to you."

"That was thoughtful. They're good kids," he said carefully.

The ball was in her court. If she wanted to see him, she was going to have to ask.

"I could mail it."

His back straightened. "Fine." He rattled off his address and was about to make an excuse to get off the phone when she spoke again.

"I'd rather you came for it yourself."

Finally. Chase hoped she couldn't hear his sigh of relief. "When?"

"Whenever it's convenient for you." She sounded unsure of herself, as though she already regretted the invitation.

"If you want, you could leave it on your porch and I could pick it up sometime."

"No." Her objection came fast enough to lend him hope. "Tomorrow," she suggested. "Or tonight, whichever you prefer."

"I'll have to check my schedule." He didn't know why he felt it was necessary to continue this pretense but he felt obliged to do so.

"I can wait."

He pressed the receiver to his chest and silently counted to ten, feeling like the biggest fool who'd ever roamed the earth.

"This afternoon looks like it would be the best. Say an hour?"

"That would be fine. I'll look for you then."

Chase waited until he heard the click of the receiver before he tossed the phone in the air and deftly caught it with one hand behind his back. "Hot damn," he shouted loudly enough to send Sandra running into the room.

"Is everything all right?"

"Everything, my dear Sandra, is just fine." He waltzed her across the room, planting a kiss on her cheek before hurrying out of the suite.

For the second time, Lesley fluffed up the decorator pillows at the end of her sofa. Holding one to her stomach, she exhaled slowly, praying she was doing the right thing.

The doorbell chimed and she must have leapt a good five inches off the ground. It was early, too early for Chase. She opened the door to find Daisy standing on the other side.

"He's coming?"

"Yes, how'd you know?"

Daisy laughed. "You wouldn't dress up like that for me."

"It's too much, isn't it?" She'd carefully gone through her wardrobe, choosing beige silk pants, a cream-colored top and a soft coral blazer. Her silver earrings were crescent-shaped and the pendant dangling from her gold chain was a gold-edged magnifying glass.

"You look fabulous, darling," Daisy commented in a lazy drawl. "Just fab-u-lous."

"Am I being too obvious?"

"Honey, compared to me, you're extremely subtle. Just be yourself and you'll do fine." She walked around the coffee table and eyed the cheese-and-cracker tray.

"What do you think?"

Daisy shrugged. "It's a nice touch."

"I've got wine cooling in the kitchen. I don't look too eager, do I?"

"No."

"You're sure?" Lesley had never been less certain of anything. Her nerves were shattered, her composure crumbling and her self-confidence was at its lowest ebb.

"There must be something in the air," Daisy said, reaching for a cracker. She was about to dip it in the nut-rolled cheddar cheese ball when Lesley slapped her hand.

"That's for Chase."

"Okay, okay." But Daisy ate the cracker anyway. "Didn't you tell me your friend Lori is getting married?" she asked.

"Yes."

Daisy relaxed on the sofa and crossed her legs, swinging one foot dangerously close to the cheese. "You'll never guess who's been calling."

"Who?"

"Charlie Glenn. He asked me out on a date. Charlie and me? He shocked me so bad I said yes without even thinking. It's been so long since someone who wasn't half bombed asked me out that I didn't know what to say."

"I've thought for weeks that Charlie's interested in you."

Daisy flapped her hand at Lesley. "Get outta here!"

"I'm serious," Lesley insisted.

"Well, that's why I think there must be something in the air. First you meet Chase, then Lori and Larry decide to tie the knot and then Charlie asks me out."

Lesley smiled. Since her divorce, Daisy had sworn off men. To the best of Lesley's knowledge, her neighbor hadn't dated since she'd separated from her ex.

"Where's Charlie taking you?"

"Taking *us*. He included the boys. We're going to Wild Waves. Eric and Kevin are ecstatic. Did you know Charlie's been married before? I didn't, and it came as a total shock to me. He never mentioned he had a kid, either. His son's a couple of years older than Eric and he wants the five of us to get together."

"I think that's wonderful."

"Yeah, I guess I do, too, but you know, I'm a little surprised. I'd never thought about Charlie in a romantic way, but I'm beginning to think I might be able to. I'm not rushing into anything, mind you, and neither is he. We've both been burned and neither of us is willing to walk through fire a second time." Daisy grabbed a second cracker. "Here I am jabbering away as though Charlie asked me to marry him or something. It's just a date. I have to keep telling myself that."

"I think Charlie's great."

"He's got a soft spot where his heart's supposed to be."

Lesley recalled how the bartender had given her a drink on the house the night Tony broke their engagement. She'd walked the streets for hours and finally landed in the cocktail lounge where Daisy worked weekends as a waitress and Charlie tended bar. Because she hadn't eaten and so rarely drank hard liquor, one stiff whiskey had Lesley feeling more than a little inebriated. Charlie had half carried her to Daisy's car, she remembered. His touch was gentle and his words soothing, although for the life of her she couldn't recall a word he'd said.

"Let me know what happens," Daisy said, uncrossing her legs and bounding off the sofa. She walked to the door and opened it, then turned around. "You're *sure* you know what you're doing?"

"No!" she cried. She wasn't sure of anything at the moment except the knot in her stomach.

"I'll do my best to keep the boys out of your hair but they're anxious to see Chase again. He certainly made an impression on those two," she said with a smile. She left, closing the door quietly behind her.

Lesley didn't blame them. Chase had treated them with compassion and kindness; not only that, he knew how to entertain them.

The phone rang then, and Lesley glared at it. She let the answering machine take the calls most of the time now, since there was always a chance the caller could be Tony. She needed to invest in call display, she told herself. It had been pure luck that she'd picked up when Chase phoned. Her reaction had been instinctive, but she was pleased she'd answered because the caller had been Chase.

The phone rang again and the machine automatically went on after the third ring. Whoever was calling didn't listen to her message and disconnected.

A moment later, she heard the doorbell. It had to be Chase. She inhaled a calming breath, squared her shoulders and crossed the room.

With a smile firmly in place, she opened the door.

"Hello, Lesley."

"Hello," she said, stepping aside for Chase to enter. "Come in, please."

He hadn't taken his eyes off her, which was both reassuring and disconcerting.

"I'm glad you could come."

"Thank you for inviting me."

How stiff they were with each other, how awkward, like polite strangers. "Sit down," she said, gesturing toward the sofa.

Chase took a seat and looked appreciatively at the cheese and crackers.

"Would you like a drink?" she asked. "I have a bottle of pinot grigio, if you'd care for that. There's a pot of coffee, too, if you'd prefer something hot."

"Wine would be nice."

"I thought so, too," she said eagerly, smiling. She moved into the kitchen, and Chase followed her.

"Do you need any help opening the wine?"

"No, I'm fine, thanks." A smaller, daintier woman might have trouble removing a cork, but she was perfectly capable of handling it. He watched her expertly open the bottle and fill two wineglasses.

"You mentioned the boys' letter," Chase said. Their thank-you note had been an excuse to contact him and they both knew it.

"I'll get it for you," she said, leaving him briefly while she retrieved the note. "They really are grateful for the time you spent with them."

He read it over, grinning, and handed it to her to read. Eric had written the short but enthusiastic message, and Kevin had decorated the handmade card with different colored fish in odd shapes and sizes.

"So," Lesley said, leading the way back into the living room. "How's it going?"

"Okay." He sat next to her on the sofa. "How about you?"

"Same."

Chase studied her. "Are you going to tell me what Tony wanted or are you going to make me guess?"

"I don't know," she answered, sipping her wine. She hoped he didn't detect the slight shake in her hand.

"You don't know if you're going to

tell me or if you're going to make me guess?"

She shook her head. "No. I don't know what he wanted. I didn't return his call."

This seemed to surprise Chase. "Why didn't you?"

Lesley raised one shoulder in a shrug. "I couldn't see that it would do either of us any good."

"You were afraid to, weren't you?"

"Yes," she admitted in a husky murmur. "I was afraid."

"Is that why you contacted me?"

"Yes." He wanted his proverbial pound of flesh, she realized, and at the same moment knew she'd give it to him. "But I don't love you, Chase."

"It's a bit difficult to care for someone like me when your heart belongs to another man." After a significant pause, he added, "A married man."

He made it sound so cold, so . . . ugly.

"He wasn't married when I fell in love with him," she said, defending herself.

"He is now."

"I don't need you to remind me of that," she cried, raising her voice for the first time.

"Good," he said brusquely.

"How are the interviews going?" she asked, hoping to make light conversation and gain the information she needed.

"All right." He set the wineglass aside as if preparing to leave.

"Would you be willing to look at another application?"

"Probably not." He stood and shoved his hands deep in his pants pockets. "I've got more than I can deal with now. Are you going to recommend a friend of yours?"

"No." Lesley closed her eyes and forced herself to continue. "I was hoping you'd consider marrying me."

Seven

"You?" Chase repeated slowly, unsure he'd heard her correctly. It seemed too good to be true, something he dared not believe.

"Yes." Lesley was standing now, too, her steady gaze nearly level with his own. She studied him as closely as he was studying her. "I'd be willing to marry you."

"Why?" Fool that he was, he had to ask, although he was confident he knew her answer. He wondered if she'd be honest enough to admit it.

"I like you very much," she said,

240

obviously choosing her words with care. "And it's clear that there's a physical attraction between us. I don't usually respond to a man the way I have to you."

He gave her no reassurances nor did he discourage her. She seemed nervous, understandably so. "Those are the only reasons?" he pressed.

"No." She was irritated with him now and he felt relieved. The more emotion she revealed the better. "I don't want to live in Seattle any longer."

She'd disappointed him. "If that's all you want, isn't marrying a man you don't love a little drastic? All you need to do is apply for a teaching position elsewhere. I'm not up on these things, but I seem to remember hearing that teachers were in high demand in a number of states. Try Montana. That's where your mother's living, isn't it?"

"I don't want to move to Montana. I'd rather be in Alaska with you."

"You still haven't answered my question."

"You're going to make me say it, aren't you? You'd like to see me humiliate myself, but I'm not going to. Now, do you want to marry me or not?"

There'd never been a single doubt in Chase's mind. He knew exactly what he wanted and he had from the beginning. He wanted Lesley. He'd always wanted Lesley, and that wasn't going to change.

"It's Tony, isn't it?" he said, as unemotionally as he could. Funny, he'd never met the man but he despised him for what he'd done to Lesley and for the way he was treating his wife. "You're afraid he has the power to reduce you to something you find abhorrent. He wants you, doesn't he? But he's married and that means you'd be his mistress and you're scared out of your wits that you'll do it because you love him."

"Yes. Yes!" Angry tears glistened in her eyes and her hands were clenched into tight fists at her sides.

"You think marrying me and moving to Alaska is the answer to all your problems."

"Yes," she cried again. "I've never lied to you, Chase, not even when it would've been convenient. You know exactly what you're getting with me."

"Yes, I do," he answered softly.

"Well?" she asked with an indignant tilt of her chin. "Are you going to marry me or not?"

"Is this a take-it-or-leave-it proposition?"

"Yes."

"All right," he said, walking away from her. "We'll be married Wednesday evening."

"Next week!" She sounded as if that was impossible. Unthinkable. "I can't put together a wedding in that amount of time. My mother and Ken are traveling in their trailer this summer and —"

"Do you want them at the ceremony?" he interrupted.

"Yes, but . . . not if it means ruining their vacation."

"Then we won't tell them until they're home." If Lesley was looking for solutions, he'd willingly supply them.

"I'd like to try calling them. And I want to invite a few friends and have a small reception."

"Fine with me. The hotel can arrange whatever you want with twenty-four hours' notice. We'll talk to them on Monday." Chase didn't intend to give her any more time than that or she might well talk herself out of it.

"What about the invitations?"

"Well, there's always email."

"No, I want real invitations."

"I'll have a messenger service hand-deliver them."

"But they'll need to be printed, and . . . oh, Chase, there are so many things to do. I have a dress, but I don't know if you'd want me to wear it since I bought it for another man, but it's so beautiful and — no, I couldn't possibly wear it, and that means I'll have to buy another one. But it took me weeks to find the *first* one."

Chase held his breath until his chest ached with the effort. "It seems to me you're looking for excuses."

"I'm not! I swear I'm not. It's just that . . ."

"Be very sure, Lesley, because once we say those vows we're married, and I take that very seriously. I assume you do, too."

She nodded slowly. "What about all my things? What will I do with them? I can't cram everything I own in a couple of suitcases."

"Pack what you want and I'll have the rest shipped. You won't need the furniture, so either sell it or give it away — whatever you want."

She took a deep breath. "Okay."

"We'll need to apply for the wedding license tomorrow morning. I'll be here by ten to pick you up," he said.

She nodded again and he started for the door.

"Chase."

He turned around, impatient now and not understanding why. Lesley had agreed to marry him, which was more than he'd expected. "Yes?"

"Would you mind kissing me?" Her voice was small and uncertain. He purposely hadn't made this easy on her for the simple reason that he wanted her to know her own mind. To be satisfied that marriage to him was the right decision. He would've liked to kiss her, and use their mutual attraction to convince her, but he couldn't. That would have felt unethical to him.

He saw that Lesley had taken several steps toward him; the least he could do was meet her halfway. She needed reassurance and he should have given it to her long before now.

He walked back to her, held her face in his hands and kissed her. The kiss deepened and deepened until Chase's control teetered precariously.

He'd forgotten exactly how good she felt in his arms. It shouldn't be like this. His experience might not have been as extensive as that of some men, but with other women he'd always been composed and in control. His response to Lesley worried him. The fact that he found her so desirable was important, but that he could so easily lose his head over her was a negative.

Lesley exhaled, that soft womanly sigh that drove him to distraction. He lifted his mouth from hers and concentrated on the nape of her neck, scattering kisses there while struggling with his own composure.

"Thank you," she whispered. The beauty of her words and the sweetness of her mouth were fatal to his control.

"This will be a real marriage, Lesley," he warned.

"I realize that." She sounded slightly offended, but Chase refused to leave any room for doubt.

"Good. I'll pick you up tomorrow morning, then."

Lesley nodded and Chase felt a

sense of victory, hollow though it was. She'd agreed to marry him, but for none of the reasons he would've liked. She was running away from a painful situation that could only bring her heartache.

He was the lesser of two evils.

Not the most solid foundation for a marriage. But time and patience and love were the mortar that would strengthen it.

"You're getting married!" Lori and Jo Ann repeated together in stunned disbelief.

"I didn't offer to buy you lunch in a fancy restaurant for nothing," Lesley commented brightly, forking up a slice of chicken in her chicken-and-spinach salad. "What are you two doing Wednesday evening?"

"Ah . . . nothing," Lori murmured.

"Not a thing," Jo Ann said.

"Great, I'd like you both to stand up for me at my wedding. Chase and I are —"

"Chase?" Jo Ann broke in. "Who on earth is Chase?"

"I didn't know you were dating anyone," Lori said, sounding more surprised than upset.

Neither of her friends had touched their seafood salads. They sat like mannequins, staring at Lesley as if she'd announced she was an escaped convict.

"Chase Goodman," Lesley repeated casually between bites. "That's the man I'm marrying."

Lori, small and fawnlike, with large dark eyes, gnawed on her lower lip. "Why does that name sound familiar?

Do I know him?"

"I doubt it. Chase's from Alaska."

"Alaska." Jo Ann said the name of the state in a low voice, as if trying to remember something. She picked up her fork. "Speaking of Alaska . . . Did either of you see the news story last week about this guy who came down from Alaska and advertised for a —" She stopped, her eyes widening. She made a few odd sounds, but nothing that resembled intelligible words.

"You're marrying the guy who advertised for a wife?" Lori looked from Lesley to Jo Ann and back again.

"Lesley, have you lost your mind?" Jo Ann finally sputtered.

"Maybe." She wasn't going to argue with her two best friends. A week earlier she'd thought the whole idea of marrying a stranger was crazy.

She'd said as much to Chase, belittled the women who'd applied, even made derogatory remarks about the type of man who'd defy convention in such an outlandish manner.

One week later, she'd agreed to be his bride.

"You *will* be my bridesmaids, won't you?"

"Of course, but —"

"No buts. The wedding's on Wednesday. I don't have time for arguments, and please, don't try to talk me out of this because you can't. Chase and I are leaving for our honeymoon after the wedding." She smiled. "The location's a surprise. After that, we're heading to Twin Creeks where Chase lives. He has to be on the job in eight days and that doesn't leave us much time."

"Pinch me," Lori said to Jo Ann, "because this doesn't seem real. We're not actually hearing this, are we? Lesley, this isn't like you."

Jo Ann shook her head and added, "It's because of Tony, isn't it? You're far too sensible to do something like this otherwise."

"I wasn't going to say anything." Lori looked down, rearranging the salt and pepper shakers on the cream-colored tablecloth. "But . . . Tony phoned me. He's worried about you, Les. He said he's been trying to get in touch with you, but you weren't returning his calls."

"Tony's been calling you?" Jo Ann sounded outraged. "Does April know about this?"

"She's out of town."

"That creep!"

"I knew when he married April that it wouldn't last," Lori said with a hint of self-righteousness.

Lesley laughed, grateful for her friends' loyalty. "You suspected it wouldn't last because Tony wasn't marrying me. If he had, you would both have been singing his praises."

"I'm beginning to think Daisy might be right about him," Jo Ann said, stabbing her fork into some crabmeat. "How could she see through him so quickly? The three of us work with the guy nine months out of the year and we have to be hit over the head before it dawns on us that Tony isn't playing fair."

"What did you tell Tony about me?" Lesley inquired casually, although her interest was anything but casual.

"Nothing much, just that I'd talked

to you recently and you sounded happy.

"He seemed surprised to hear that and said he was afraid you were depressed and avoiding people. He acted concerned and guilty about the way he'd hurt you. I . . ."

"Yes?" Lesley prompted.

"I felt sorry for him by the time we hung up."

"*Sorry* for him?" Jo Ann asked, incredulous. "Why would you feel sorry for Tony? He's the one who broke Lesley's heart and married someone else."

Lori shrugged, looking mildly guilty herself. "He didn't actually say so, but I had the feeling he regrets marrying April." Lori paused, frowning. "She's never been very friendly toward the three of us, has she?"

"Who can blame her for being un-friendly?" Lesley was the first one to defend April.

"Tony made her situation impossible at school," Lori agreed. "We did our best to make her feel welcome, but we'd all worked with Lesley and April knew that. She attended hardly any faculty functions after the wedding. I'll bet she's really a nice person, and we'd find that out if she ever gave anyone the chance to know her."

"She gave Tony plenty of chances," Jo Ann muttered, unwilling even now to forget the upheaval the new first-grade teacher had brought into their lives.

"You haven't talked to Tony yourself?" Lori asked, ignoring Jo Ann's pettiness. For that, Lesley was grateful.

"Not since school got out." She felt good about resisting the temptation to phone him, but it had exacted a high emotional price. "I won't, either," she said, her resolve growing stronger.

Jo Ann nodded vigorously. Lori looked uncertain.

"Aren't you curious about what he wants?"

"Come on, Lori. What do you *think* Tony wants?" Jo Ann asked.

Lori studied her for a disbelieving moment. "You don't really believe that, do you?"

"Lori, wake up!" Jo Ann said sarcastically and snapped her fingers. "When a married man phones another woman — his ex-fiancée, no less — while his wife's out of town, there's only one reason."

"I hate to think Tony would do that."

Lesley felt the same way, but she couldn't allow her tenderness for Tony to mislead her.

"Stop." Jo Ann raised both hands. "We've strayed from the real subject here and that's Lesley's wedding."

" 'Lesley's wedding,' " Lori echoed, sending a dismayed glance at Jo Ann. "Are you in love with Chase?" she asked.

"No." Lesley refused to be anything but honest with her friends. When she'd told her mother and Ken she'd stretched the truth, subtly of course, but she'd never be able to fool her friends. Her mother was another story; she believed Lesley was in love because that was what she wanted to believe.

Lori's jaw fell open. "You don't even love him."

"I've only known the man for a little more than one week. It's a bit difficult to develop a deep, emotional attachment in that length of time."

"You're willing to marry him anyway," Jo Ann murmured thoughtfully. "That tells me a lot. He's obviously got something going for him."

"He's good with kids, and he's kind. And brave," she said, remembering his pursuit of her mugger. Those were only three of Chase's character traits that appealed to her. Honesty was another.

"What's he look like?" Lori was eager to know.

"Kind of like you'd expect someone from Alaska to look. He's tall and muscular and his eyes are a lovely deep brown. He's a comfortable sort of person to be with, entertaining and funny. When he laughs it comes from his belly."

"You're marrying a man because of the way he laughs?"

It sounded absurd, but in part she was. Chase had a wonderful sense of humor and Lesley found that quality important in any relationship, but vital in a marriage.

"You really like this guy, don't you?"

Lesley nodded. It surprised her how much she did.

"Would you guys have time to shop with me this afternoon?" Lesley asked, ending her introspection. She hadn't said a word about the way Chase kissed. He should win awards for his style. She'd never known a man could arouse such a heated reaction with a few kisses.

"You're going through with this, aren't you?" Even now Lori didn't quite seem to believe it.

"Yes, I am." She turned to Jo Ann, expecting an argument, unsought advice or words of caution.

"I almost envy you," Jo Ann remarked instead. "This is going to be an incredible adventure. You'll email us and let us know what happens, won't you?"

Lesley laughed, astonished when she felt tears gather in her eyes. Through all the pain and difficulties of the past year, she'd been blessed with truly good friends.

"I wonder what Alaska will be like," Lori said dreamily. "Do you think Twin Creeks will have a friendly moose wandering through town like in the opening of that old TV show?"

"Hi," Lesley said, letting herself into the house. Chase had spent the afternoon at her rented home, supervising the packers so her personal things would be ready for shipping.

He tossed aside the magazine he was reading and smiled up at her with that roguish gleam in his eyes. Her heart reacted with a surprising surge of warmth.

"How'd your meeting with your friends go?" Chase asked.

"Really well." It was ridiculous to be shy with him now.

"They didn't try to talk you out of the wedding?"

Lesley grinned as she sat down on the sofa that would soon belong to Daisy and her boys. "I'll admit they were shocked, but once I told them what a fabulous kisser you are, they were green with envy."

"You aren't going to change your mind, are you?"

Lori and Jo Ann had asked her that question, too, and she gave him the same answer. "No. Are you worried?"

"Yes." His voice was gruff and he reached for her, kissing her hungrily.

Lesley could find no will to resist him. He'd only kissed her once since she'd agreed to be his wife and she needed his touch, longed for it. She leaned forward and braced her hand against his chest. The strong, even feel of his pulse reassured her that he enjoyed their kisses as much as she did. At least she wasn't alone in this.

Chase took hold of her waist and pulled her closer. His kiss was slow, deep and thorough. And not nearly enough.

Chase started to pull away and she protested. "No . . ."

His mouth came back to hers once more. By the time Chase pulled away from her, she was weak and dizzy and breathless.

"Lesley, listen," he whispered, pressing his forehead to hers.

"No," she whispered back. "Just hold me for a few minutes. Please." She didn't want to talk, not then, nor was she interested in thinking because if she analyzed what she was doing, she might change her mind, after all.

All Lesley wanted was to *feel.* When she was in Chase's arms she could feel again. For months she'd been trapped in a kind of numbness.

Sometimes the pain surged up to inundate her but most of the time she'd felt nothing. No laughter. No tears. Just a lethargy that sapped away her energy and destroyed her dreams.

Then she'd met Chase and suddenly she was laughing again, dreaming again. Whenever he kissed her, a cascade of feelings flooded her body — and her heart. She needed to experience that excitement, those emotions.

For reasons of his own, Chase needed her, too. She would reciprocate generously and without reserve because she wanted him as badly as he wanted her.

As she luxuriated in the shelter of his arms, he buried his face in her neck, his breathing heavy.

Then, without warning, he broke away from her, leaving her breathless. Stunned. Before she could analyze what was happening, he was on his feet and moving toward the door. "I have to go."

"Go? But why?"

He paused, his back to her. "Because if I stay we're going to end up in bed."

"You . . . you don't want to be with me?"

Chase didn't answer. Although Lesley thought she knew why he'd resisted the temptation to make love to her, she still felt hurt. She suspected that he feared she might not go through with the marriage. His lack of trust offended her, and his rejection was more than insulting, it was painful in a way that echoed past anguish. She'd lowered her guard, offered him everything she had to give and he was walking away from her. The six-year-old child whose father had abandoned her was back, chanting her fears.

"Go, then," she said furiously, trying to silence the sounds of grief only she could hear.

He paused at the front door, his shoulders slumped forward. "I can't leave you now."

"Sure you can."

He turned back and walked over to the sofa, sitting down next to her. He pulled her into his arms, disregarding her token objections, and held her. She let him, although the little girl in her wanted to push him away, hurt him for hurting her. But the womanly part of her needed his comfort.

As Chase kissed the crown of her head, she sighed and nestled in his arms.

"You tempt me, Lesley Campbell, more than any woman I've ever known," he whispered.

"You tempt me, too."

She felt his smile and was glad he was there with her.

"Becky Bright, the reporter who did that interview with me, phoned earlier this afternoon," he told her.

"How come?"

"She wants to do an interview with the two of us right after the wedding. Do you mind?"

"I suppose not. Do you?"

"I do, but it's the only way I can think of to stop the phone calls. According to the answering service, they're still coming in."

"Still?"

"I had the billboard taken down and asked Sandra to cancel all the remaining appointments, but there are more women phoning now than ever. I'm sure some called before and were discouraged when they didn't hear back right away. Several were phoning to see if I'd made a decision and others wanted to know it if was too late."

"It's certainly been an . . . interesting experiment, hasn't it?" she said.

"Yes, but it isn't one I care to repeat."

Lesley jabbed him with her elbow. "I should hope not!"

Chase laughed, slid his arms around her waist and nuzzled her neck. "I'm going to have my hands full with one wife."

"What about the applicants you've already seen?"

"I had Sandra write up a form letter and send it out to everyone, including them."

"To eight hundred women."

Lesley felt his smile against her skin. "Not exactly."

"What do you mean?"

"I got eight hundred calls, yes — well, maybe a thousand in total if we add the recent ones — but not all of them were from women who wanted to be my wife. I found that at least a hundred were from mothers planning to introduce me to their daughters."

Lesley stared at him. "I hope you're joking."

"I'm not. And there were more crank calls than I care to mention."

"So," Lesley said, feeling a bit

cocky. "When you come right down to it, exactly how many serious applications did you receive?"

"One."

"One? But you said . . . I heard on the news —"

"Yours was the only one I took seriously."

His words were sweet and soft and precisely what she needed. She rewarded him by throwing her arms around his neck and directing his mouth to hers. Their kisses were slow and lazy and pleasurable.

Chase wasn't ready to leave for another hour. He needed to finish up some last-minute details with the answering service and the billboard company. After that, she lingered with him on the front porch for ten minutes, neither of them eager to separate even for a few hours.

"I'll be back soon," he promised. "Where would you like to have dinner?"

Lesley smiled. "Are you in the mood for another hamburger and a rematch at the golf course?"

"You're on."

Lesley stood on the porch until his car was out of sight. She glanced at her watch and realized that in twenty-four hours they'd be married.

The house felt empty without Chase. In fact, not just her house but her whole life felt different now that she was marrying him.

She showered and changed clothes, and was packing her suitcase when the doorbell chimed. Her steps were eager as she ran across the living room. Chase could come in without the formality of waiting for her to answer the door. She should have said as much.

Her smile bright, she opened the door.

"Hello, Lesley."

Her heart, which had seemed light only seconds before, plummeted like a deadweight to the pit of her stomach.

"Hello, Tony."

EIGHT

"Lesley, oh, Lesley." Tony's hands reached for hers, gripping them tightly. "You don't have any idea how good it is to see you again. I've been desperate to talk to you. Why didn't you return my calls?"

The immediate attraction was there, the way it had always been. That shouldn't have surprised her, but it did. Lesley had hoped that when she saw Tony again, she wouldn't experience this terrible need.

She jerked her hands free.

"Lesley." Tony's eyes widened with

275

hurt disbelief.

"I didn't return your calls for a reason. We don't have anything to discuss."

"That's where you're wrong. Lesley, my love —"

"I'm not your love."

"But you are," he said in a hurt-little-boy manner. "You'll always be my love . . . you always have been."

"You're married to April." He obviously needed to be reminded of that, and so did she. The strength of her love for him, despite his marital status, was nearly overwhelming. All the feelings she'd struggled to vanquish threatened her now.

"I know . . . I know." He sounded sad and uncertain, a combination that never failed to touch her heart. Part of her longed to invite him into her home and listen to his troubles, but she dared not and knew it.

"I'm making a new life for myself," she insisted, steeling herself against the pleading in his eyes. "I've given notice to the school and to my landlord."

"A new life? One without me?"

"Yes. Please, Tony, just leave." She stepped back, intending to close the door, but he placed his foot over the threshold, blocking her attempt.

"I can't," he said. "Not until I've talked to you."

"Tony, please." This was so much harder than she'd imagined it would be. He must have sensed that because he edged closer.

"Tony." Her voice shook with the force of her desperation. "We have nothing to say to each other."

"Lesley."

Chase's voice sounded like an angel's harp. She was so grateful he'd arrived that she nearly burst into tears.

"Chase," she said, breaking away from Tony and rushing forward. She must have appeared desperate, but she didn't care. Chase was her one link to sanity and she held on to him with both hands.

"What's going on here?" Tony demanded. "Who is this man?"

"Actually, I was about to ask you the same thing," Chase said stiffly.

"I'm Tony Field."

Lesley felt Chase stiffen as soon as he recognized the name. He reacted by placing his arm possessively around Lesley's shoulders and pulling her closer to his side.

"Who *is* this man?" Tony asked again.

Lesley opened her mouth to explain, but before she could utter a single word, Chase spoke.

"Lesley and I are going to be married."

"Married?" Tony laughed as if he'd just heard a good joke. "You can't be serious."

"We're dead serious," Chase responded.

"Lesley?" Tony looked at her, clearly expecting her to deny it.

"It's true," she said with as much conviction as she could manage.

"That's ridiculous. You've never mentioned anyone named Chase and I know for a fact that you weren't dating him before school was out. Isn't this rather sudden?"

"Not in the least," Chase said as if they'd been involved for years.

"Lesley?"

"There's a lot you don't know about my fiancée," Chase said, smiling down at her.

It was all Lesley could do not to tell them both to stop playing these ridiculous games. Tony regarded her with a tormented expression, as though *he* was the loyal one and she'd betrayed him. Chase wasn't any better. The full plumage of his male pride was fanned out in opulent display.

"You can't possibly be marrying this man," Tony said, ignoring Chase and concentrating on her instead.

"I already said I was." She hated the way her voice quavered. Chase didn't seem pleased with the lack of enthusiasm in her trembling response, but that couldn't be helped.

"The ceremony's tomorrow evening," Chase added.

"Lesley, you don't love this man," Tony continued, his gaze burning into hers.

"You don't know that," Chase challenged.

"I do know it. Lesley loves *me*. Tell him, sweetheart. You'd be doing us both a grave disservice if you didn't tell him the truth."

Lesley could see no reason to confess the obvious. "I'm marrying Chase."

"But you love me," Tony insisted, his voice agitated. She noticed that he clenched his fists at his sides as if his temper was about to explode. He'd fight for her if necessary, he seemed to be saying.

"You're already married," Chase told Tony with evident delight.

Tony turned to Lesley once more, ignoring Chase. "Marrying April was a mistake. That's what I've been trying to tell you. If only you'd returned my calls . . . I love you, Lesley. I have for years. I don't know what came over me. . . . I can see now that April and I were never right for each other. I've been miserable without you."

"You don't need to listen to this," Chase hissed in her ear. He tried to steer her past Tony and toward the front door, but she was rooted to the spot and unable to move.

"You've got to listen," Tony pleaded, "before you ruin both our lives."

"Where's April now?" Chase asked.

"She left me."

"You're lying." Chase's voice was tight with barely restrained anger. "You said she was visiting her mother for a week."

"She phoned and told me she's not coming back. She knows I love Lesley and she can't live with that anymore. It's a blessing to us all."

"If you believe him," Chase said to Lesley, "there's a bridge in Brooklyn you might be interested in buying."

"I'm telling you the truth," Tony insisted. "I should never have married April. It was a mistake on both our parts. April knows how I feel about you. She's always known. I can't go on pretending anymore. April can't, either. That's why she went to visit her mother and why she's decided not to come back."

"I'm marrying Chase." Her voice wavered, but not her certainty. She couldn't trust Tony, couldn't believe him. Chase was right about that. He'd lied to her before, and the experience had taught her painful but valuable lessons.

"Lesley, don't," Tony cried. "I'm pleading with you. Don't do something you'll regret the rest of our lives. I made a terrible mistake. Don't compound it by making another."

"She doesn't believe you any more than I do," Chase said calmly.

"The least you can do is have the decency to give us some privacy," Tony shouted, frustrated and short-tempered.

"Not on your life."

"You're afraid, aren't you?" Tony shouted. "Because Lesley loves me and you know it. You think if you can keep her from listening to me, she'll go through with the wedding, but you're wrong. She doesn't need you, not when she's got me."

"But she *hasn't* got you. In case you've forgotten, I'll remind you again — you're married."

As he was talking, Tony stepped closer to Chase, his stance challenging.

Chase dropped his arm from Lesley's shoulders and moved toward Tony. The two men were practically chest to chest. It wouldn't take much for the situation to erupt into a brawl.

"Stop it, both of you!" Lesley yelled. She was surprised none of the neighbors were out yet to watch the show. "This is ridiculous."

"You love me," Tony said. "You

can't marry this . . . this barbarian."

"Just watch her," Chase returned with a wide smile.

"I'm not doing *anything* until both of you stop behaving like six-year-olds," Lesley said. "I can't believe either one of you would resort to this childish behavior."

"I'll divorce April," Tony promised. "I swear by everything I hold dear that I'll get her out of my life."

"I'd think a husband would hold his *wife* dear," Chase said. "Apparently that isn't so. Your vows meant nothing the first time. What makes you so sure they'll mean any more on a second go-round?"

"I'm trying to be as civil as I can," Tony muttered, "but if you want to fight this out, fine."

"Anytime," Chase said, grinning

broadly as if he welcomed the con-frontation, "anyplace."

"Fine."

They were chest to chest once more.

Lesley managed to wedge herself between them and braced a hand against each of their chests. "I think you should go," she said to Tony. It was useless to try to discuss anything now. She wanted to believe him, but Chase was right. The first message Tony had left claimed that April was away for a week visiting her mother. He hadn't said a word about his marriage being a mistake or that he still cared for her.

"I'm not leaving you, not when you're making the biggest mistake of your life," Tony told her. "I already said I'd divorce April. What more do you want me to do? The marriage was a mistake from the first! What else can I do? Tell me, Lesley, tell me and I'll do whatever it takes to make amends to you."

"I believe the lady asked you to leave," Chase said with the same easy grace. "That's all she wants from you. Get out of her life."

"No."

"It'll give me a good deal of pleasure to assist you."

The next thing she knew, Chase had grabbed Tony's arm and steered him toward his parked car.

Lesley stood on the porch, her teeth sinking into her lower lip as she watched the unpleasant scene. She was furious and didn't know who with — Chase or Tony. Both had behaved like children fighting on the playground. Neither of them had shown any maturity in dealing with an awkward situation.

The two men exchanged a few words at Tony's vehicle and it looked for a moment as if a fistfight was about to erupt. In the end, Tony climbed inside his car and drove away.

Lesley was pacing her living room when Chase entered the house. "How *could* you?" she demanded.

"How could I what? Treat lover boy the way he deserved, you mean?"

"You weren't any better than he was! I expected more from you, Chase. The least you could've done was . . . was be civil about the whole thing. Instead you acted like a jealous lover." She continued pacing. Her anger had created an energy within her that couldn't be ignored.

"Did you want to talk to him alone?"

"No."

"Then what *did* you expect me to do?"

"I don't know," she said. "Something different than strong-arming him."

"You sound like you wanted to invite him in for tea and then sit around discussing this like civilized adults."

"Yes!" she cried. "That would've been better than a shouting match on my front porch. The two of you behaved as though I was a prize baseball card you both wanted. Tony had traded me away and now he wants me back and you weren't about to see that happen."

Chase went still. "Is that what *you* wanted?" he asked. "To be handed back to Tony?"

"No, of course it isn't!"

"He can't stand the thought of losing you."

"He's the one who ended the relationship, not me. It's over, Chase."

Chase walked to the window and stared outside. He didn't speak for a long time and seemed to be weighing his thoughts.

"You . . . you told me once that you had a problem with a woman playing one man against another," she said. "I'm not doing that, Chase. I wouldn't. You're the man I'm marrying, not Tony."

"You love him," Chase said, turning to face her, "although he doesn't deserve your devotion. You could have lied to me about your feelings, but you haven't and I'm grateful."

"I don't trust Tony," she said, "but I trust you."

"You might not trust him, but you *want* to believe him, don't you?"

"I . . . I don't know. It doesn't matter if I do, does it? I've already agreed to marry you, and I'm not backing out." She refused to do to Chase what Tony had done to her. She wouldn't push him aside in favor of Tony's promises. Chase was right; Tony had always been a sore loser, no matter what the stakes.

Chase said nothing for several minutes. "The choice is yours," he finally said, "and I'll abide by whatever you decide. I want you, Lesley. Don't misunderstand me. I'm surprised by how much I desire you. If you agree to marry me, I promise you I'll do my best to be a good husband."

"You make it sound like I haven't made up my mind. I've already told you — and Tony — that I have. I'm going through with the wedding."

"It isn't too late to call it off."

"Why would I do that?" she asked, forcing a laugh.

"Because you're in love with Tony," Chase answered with dark, sober eyes focused on her. "Think about this very carefully," he advised and walked to her door.

"You're leaving?" She was afraid Tony would return and she didn't know what she'd do if Chase wasn't there to buffer his effect on her.

"Will you call me in the morning?" he asked. He didn't need to explain what he expected to hear. That was obvious. If she was willing to go through with the ceremony, she needed to let him know.

"I can tell you that right now," she said, folding her hands in an effort to keep from reaching for him.

"You might feel differently later."

"I won't. I promise you I won't." The desperate quality of her voice was all the answer he seemed to need.

He came over to her, placed his hands on her shoulders and drew her into his arms. "I shouldn't touch you, but I can't make myself leave without kissing you goodbye. Forgive me for that, Lesley." His last words were whispered as he lowered his mouth to hers. The kiss was filled with a longing and a hunger that left her breathless and yearning for more.

He expelled his breath, then turned

and walked away.

Lesley watched him go and had the feeling she might never see him again.

Her knees were trembling and she sank onto the sofa and hid her face in her hands.

He'd lost her, Chase told himself as he unlocked the door to his hotel suite. He could've taken the advantage and run with it. At first he thought he'd do exactly that. Tony wasn't right for Lesley — anyone could see it.

Okay, he believed it so strongly because he wanted her for himself. Maybe the jerk *was* good for Lesley, although Chase couldn't see it.

Chase suspected Tony would string her along for years. He'd promise to divorce April but there'd be complications. There were always complications in cases like this, and Lesley would be completely disheartened by the time Tony was free. If he ever followed through on his promises. Chase knew exactly whose interests Tony was serving, and those were his own.

Tony might have some genuine affection for Lesley, but he didn't really love her. He couldn't possibly, otherwise he'd never put her through this agony.

Then again, Chase's own intentions weren't exactly pure, either. He needed a wife and he wanted Lesley. It didn't matter to him that she was in love with another man; all that mattered was her willingness to marry him and live with him in Alaska.

If there was a law against selfishness, he'd be swinging by his neck, right next to Tony.

So he'd done the only thing he could and still live with himself in the weeks to come. This business of being honorable was hard, much harder than he'd realized.

He'd given Lesley both the freedom and the privacy to make whatever choice she wanted. He wouldn't stand in her way, judge or condemn her if she decided not to go through with their marriage.

He was about to lose the wife he wanted, and nobility didn't offer much compensation.

All he had to do was wait until she'd made up her mind. He had the distinct feeling that this was going to be a long night.

■ ■ ■ ■

"It shouldn't be this hard," Lesley wailed to her no-nonsense neighbor.

"You're right. It shouldn't," Daisy agreed. She stood next to Lesley's refrigerator, one hand on her hip. "Look at it this way. You could let Chase go back to Alaska alone and spend the next year or two being lied to, manipulated and emotionally abused by a jerk. Or," she added with a lazy smile, "you could marry a terrific man who adores you."

"Chase doesn't adore me."

"Maybe not, but he *is* crazy about you."

"I'm not even sure that's true."

"Haven't you got eyes in your head?" Daisy asked sarcastically. "He chose you out of hundreds of women."

"Not exactly . . ."

"Listen, if you want to argue with someone, let me bring in the boys. They're much better at it than either of us. I don't have time to play silly games with you. I'm calling this the way I see it. If you want to mess up your life, that's your choice."

"I don't," Lesley insisted.

"Then why don't you phone Chase? You said he was waiting to hear from you."

"I know, but . . ."

"Is there always going to be a *but* with you?" Daisy demanded impatiently. "Now, call the man before I get really mad."

Smiling, Lesley reached for the phone. She prayed she was doing the right thing. After wrestling all night with the decision, she got up and tearfully called Daisy, sobbing out her sorry tale. Daisy, who was already late for her classes, had listened intently. She seemed to know exactly what Lesley should do. She made it all sound so straightforward, so easy. It should've been, but it wasn't, even now with the phone pressed to her ear.

"Hello."

"Chase, it's Lesley. I'm sorry to phone so early, but I thought you'd want to know as soon as possible."

There was a slight hesitation before he spoke. "It would simplify matters."

"I . . . want to go through with the marriage this evening."

"You're sure?"

He had to ask. Why couldn't he just have left it alone? "Yes, I'm sure."

Her voice shook as if she was on the verge of tears.

Daisy took the receiver from her hand. "She knows what she's doing, Chase. Now don't you worry, I'll have her to the church on time." Whatever Chase said made Daisy laugh. After a couple of minutes, she replaced the receiver. "You going to make it through the day without changing your mind?"

"I . . . don't have any choice, do I?"

"None. If you stand that man up at the altar, I'm going to murder you and marry him myself. The boys would be thrilled."

Lesley laughed. "All right. I'll see you back here at four. Don't be late, Daisy, I'm going to need all the support I can get."

"What if Tony calls you?"

"He probably will, but fortunately I don't plan on being here. I've got a million things to do and I don't intend to waste a single moment on Tony Field."

"Good." Daisy beamed her a bright smile and was out the door a moment later.

Being nervous came as a surprise to Chase. He'd expected to stand before the preacher he'd hired and repeat his vows without a qualm. He had no doubts, no regrets about making Lesley his bride. Just nerves.

When she and her close friends, including Daisy and sons, arrived at the hotel for the simple wedding ceremony, Chase hadn't been able to take his eyes off her. He'd never seen a more beautiful woman. He'd rented a tuxedo, although what had prompted that was beyond his comprehension. The tie felt like it was strangling him and the cummerbund reminded him of the time he'd broken his ribs. He knew Lesley would be pleased, though, and when she smiled at him, he was glad he'd made the effort.

She'd chosen a soft peach dress, overlaid with white lace. She didn't wear a veil but a pretty pearl headpiece with white silk flowers. The bouquet of white baby roses was clutched in her hands.

Lesley had tried to call her mother and stepfather, wherever they were, but their cell phone wasn't on. Apparently that was typical. Chase reassured her again that they'd tell them later, perhaps arrange to see them in the fall. He, too, was without family — he'd told her only that his parents had died, nothing more — so their guests were mostly Lesley's friends.

It was all rather informal. She introduced Chase to Lori and Jo Ann and a number of others, and he shook hands with each one. Minutes later, it was time for the ceremony.

They stood with everyone gathered around them in the middle of the room. The minister said a few words about marriage and its significance, then asked them to repeat their vows.

It was at that moment that Chase fully comprehended what was happening between Lesley and him. He pledged before God that he would love Lesley and meet her needs, both physical and emotional.

The responsibility weighed on his mind. He'd given Lesley time to weigh the decision before agreeing to be his bride, never dreaming *he* needed to think about it, as well.

He looked at Lesley as she said her vows. Her steady gaze met his and her voice was strong and clear, without hesitation. When it came time, he slipped the gold band on her finger. He noticed tears brightening her eyes, but her smile reassured him. He could only hope these were tears of joy and not regret.

When he received permission to kiss his bride, Chase gently took her in his arms and kissed her. With everyone watching them, he made sure it was a short but intense kiss. A kiss that went on longer than he'd planned . . .

Lesley's eyes were laughing when they broke apart. "You'll pay for that later, Chase Goodman," she promised in a fervent whisper.

Chase could hardly wait.

There was enough food to feed twice as many people as their fifty or so guests. He wasn't sure how many would be there, so he'd had the hotel staff handle everything. Lesley had given him the names of her friends and he'd invited several people, as well, including Sandra and her husband.

Becky Bright was there, along with her cameraman. Lesley was wonderful during the interview, answering Becky's questions without a hint of nervousness. He suspected it was because of her training as a teacher. Personally he was grateful she'd dealt with the reporter because he was at a loss for words.

He'd considered the ceremony itself a mere formality, something that was necessary, a legal requirement, and that was all.

Now he wasn't so sure.

The vows had gotten to him. He hadn't truly taken the seriousness of his commitment to heart until he realized that these promises were more, much more, than a few mumbled words. They were *vows*, a soul-deep contract made between Lesley and himself. A contract that affected every single part of his life.

"I've never seen a more beautiful bride," he told her while they were going through the buffet line. They hadn't had a moment alone all evening. His heart was crammed full with all the things he wanted to say to her, and couldn't.

"I've never seen a handsomer groom," she whispered back and when she looked at him, her eyes softened.

Chase filled his plate. "I meant what I said." He knew that sounded melodramatic and a little trite, but he couldn't keep it to himself any longer.

"About what?" Lesley added a cherry tomato to her plate.

"The vows. I wasn't just repeating a bunch of meaningless phrases, I meant them, Lesley. I'm going to do everything in my power to be the right kind of husband to you."

She didn't look at him, didn't move, and he wondered, briefly, if he'd frightened her with his intensity, or perhaps shocked her. "Lesley?"

"I'm sorry," she whispered brokenly, staring down at the bowl of pasta salad.

"I shouldn't have told you that." She was suffering from pangs of guilt, he reasoned. The ceremony obviously hadn't affected her the way it had him.

"No . . . Oh, Chase, that was the most beautiful thing you could've said." She raised her eyes to his and he saw she was struggling to hold back tears. "I meant it, too, every word. I'm eager to show you how good a wife I intend to be."

Until the moment Lesley had walked into the hotel that afternoon, Chase wasn't entirely convinced she'd show up for the wedding. All day he'd tried to brace himself in case she didn't. Now she was his wife, and there was no turning back for either of them.

"Where are you going for your honeymoon?" Daisy asked, filling her plate on the opposite side of the buffet table. "I meant to ask."

"Victoria," Chase answered. He hadn't said anything to Lesley, wanting to surprise her. That didn't seem important now.

"Victoria," she repeated. "Oh, Chase, what a wonderful idea."

"I don't imagine you're going to do much sightseeing, though," Daisy added with a suggestive chuckle.

"Daisy!" Lesley said as she blushed becomingly.

Their honeymoon. The words floated through his mind. Not knowing if Lesley would even be there for the wedding, he'd put off all thoughts as to what would follow.

He'd wanted to make love with Lesley almost from the moment they'd met. But he was determined not to enter into the physical side of their relationship until they were both prepared to deal with it. To accept the emotional repercussions of that aspect of their lives — of their life together. He didn't know about Lesley, but he was more than ready. He only hoped she was, too.

Their guests didn't seem in any hurry to leave. The champagne flowed freely, but Chase drank only a small amount. He needed a clear head.

They left, under a spray of rice and birdseed. He placed Lesley's suitcase in the back of his rental car and ran around to the front of the vehicle.

"Ready?" he asked, smiling over at his wife. *His wife.* The word still felt awkward in his mind. Awkward, but very right. He'd accomplished what he'd set out to do. He'd gotten himself a bride.

The one bride he'd wanted above all.

NINE

"The honeymoon suite," Lesley whispered as the bellman carried in their suitcases. "You booked us the honeymoon suite?"

Chase gave the bellman a generous tip and let him out the door. "Why are you so surprised? We're on our honeymoon, aren't we?"

"Yes, but, oh, I don't know . . ." She walked around the room and ran her hand over the plush bedspread on the king-size bed. "Oh, Chase, look," she said after she'd walked into the bathroom. "The tub's huge."

"Imagine wasting all that water," he teased, enjoying her excitement.

"They left champagne and chocolates, too."

"I'll file a complaint. How are any two people supposed to survive on that? A man needs real food."

"There's always room service."

"Right," he said, laughing. "I forgot about that."

"Oh, Chase, this is so lovely." She seemed shy about touching him, stopping just short of his arms. He was a bit embarrassed himself, although he didn't understand why. Lesley was his wife and he was her husband.

"I . . . I think I'll unpack," she said, reaching for her suitcase.

"Good idea." There was definitely something wrong with him. Lesley should be in his arms by now, begging him to make love to her. Instead, they were standing back to back emptying their suitcases, as though they had every intention of wearing all those clothes.

"Are you hungry?" he asked, just to make conversation.

"No, but if you want to order something, go ahead."

"I'm fine." No, he wasn't. His temperature was rising by the minute.

"I think I'll take a bath," she said next.

"Good idea." He realized after he spoke that she might find his enthusiasm a bit insulting, but by the time he thought to say something she was in the bathroom.

The sound of running water filled the suite. He noted that she'd left the door ajar, but he wasn't certain she'd done it on purpose.

Focusing his attention on unpacking, Chase opened and closed several drawers, but his mind wasn't on putting his clothes in any order. It was on Lesley in the other room.

Lesley removing her clothes.

Lesley stepping naked into the big tub.

Lesley sighing that soft, womanly sigh of hers as she slipped into the steaming water.

The image was so powerful that Chase sagged onto the edge of the bed. He didn't know what was the matter with him. They were married, and he was acting like a choirboy.

"Would you like me to wash your back?" he asked.

"Please."

Chase's spirits lifted. That sounded encouraging. He smoothed back his hair and rolled up his sleeves before advancing into the bathroom.

Lesley was exactly as he'd pictured her. She was lying in the tub, surrounded by frothy bubbles.

The scent of blooming roses wafted up to him, and her pink toes were perched against the far end. The welcome he saw in her eyes made his heart beat so furiously that for a moment he couldn't breathe.

He cleared his throat. "How's the water?" he asked, shoving his hands in his pants pockets.

"It's perfect."

"I see you've added a bunch of women's stuff to that water."

"Women's stuff?"

"Bubble bath or whatever."

"Do you mind?"

"Not in the least." It was driving him slowly insane, but that didn't bother him nearly as much as the view he had of her body. She raised one knee and the bubbles slid down her leg in a slow, tantalizing pattern.

Her leg was pink from the steamy water and for the life of him, he couldn't stop staring at it. For the life of him he couldn't stop thinking about that same leg wrapped around his waist. . . .

"The, uh, water looks inviting." His tongue nearly stuck to the roof of his mouth, he was so excited.

"Would you care to join me?"

His heart was doing that crazy pounding again. "You sure? I mean . . ." Darned if he knew *what* he meant. "Should I bring the champagne and chocolates?"

"Just the champagne. Let's save the chocolates for later."

He nearly stumbled out of the room in his eagerness to get her what she wanted. He opened the bottle and the popping sound echoed like a small explosion. His hands trembled as he poured them each a flute of champagne. He carried them into the other room, then handed her the glass and sipped from his own, badly needing the temporary courage it offered. Then he realized Lesley hadn't tasted hers.

"I'll wait until you're in the bath with me," she explained.

"Oh." That was when it occurred to him that he'd need to undress. He did his best not to be self-conscious, but didn't know how well he succeeded. He wasn't normally shy, but he'd lived alone for a lot of years and when he undressed there usually wasn't someone watching his every move.

He stepped into the tub and she moved forward to make room for him. He eased himself into the hot water, positioning himself behind her. She was slippery in his embrace and he tucked his arms around her waist and brought her up against him. He brushed his mouth over her hair and relaxed, closing his eyes.

"You feel good," he whispered. That had to be the understatement of the century.

Lesley had gone still and so had he. It was as though they'd both lost the need to breathe. He cupped her breasts and she sighed as if this was what she'd been waiting for, as if she wondered what had taken him so long.

Darned if he knew.

He smiled, not with amusement, but with male pride and satisfaction.

"You feel like silk," he whispered, rubbing his hand down her smooth abdomen. She turned her head toward him, inviting his kiss.

Chase didn't disappoint her. He bent forward and kissed her slowly, seducing her mouth with his own. Soon he didn't know who was seducing whom. They were both breathless by the time he lifted his head.

They kissed again, the urgency of their need centered on their mouths as she buckled beneath him, gasping and moaning.

Chase broke off the kiss. In one

swift motion he stood, taking her with him. Water sloshed over the sides of the tub, but Chase hardly noticed. He carried Lesley to the bed and placed her on it, not caring if they were soaking wet or that they'd left a watery trail.

When the loving was over, he rested his forehead against hers, his breath uneven. He could find no words to explain what had happened. No experience had ever been this intense. No woman had ever satisfied him so completely or brought him to the point of no return the way Lesley had.

Whatever was between them, be it commitment or love or something he couldn't define, it was out of his control.

Everything with Lesley was beyond his experience. Everything with her was going to be brand-new.

Butchart Gardens was breathtakingly beautiful. Chase and Lesley spent their first morning as husband and wife walking hand in hand along the meandering paths, over the footbridges and through the secret corners of the gardens. Lesley couldn't remember ever seeing any place as beautiful, with a profusion of so many varieties of flowers that she soon lost count.

By the time they stopped for lunch, Lesley was famished. Chase was, too, gauging by the amount of food he ordered.

"I've got to build my strength up," he told her.

Lesley didn't know she was still capable of blushing, not after the wondrous night they'd spent. She hadn't known it was possible for any two people to make love so fervently or so frequently. Just when she was convinced she'd never survive another burst of pleasure, he'd convince her that she could. And she did.

"You're blushing." Chase sounded shocked.

"Thank you for calling attention to it," she chided. "If one of us is blushing, it should be you."

"Me?"

She leaned across the table, not wanting anyone to overhear. "After last night," she whispered heatedly.

"What about last night?" His voice boomed like a cannon shot, or so it seemed to Lesley.

"You know," she said, sorry now for having introduced the subject.

"No, I don't. You'd better tell me."

"You're . . . a superman."

He grinned and wiggled his eyebrows suggestively.

"Chase!"

"As soon as we finish lunch, let's go back to the hotel."

"We've only seen half of the gardens," she protested, but not too strenuously.

"We'll come back tomorrow."

"It's the middle of the afternoon."

"So?"

"It's . . . early." The excuse was token at best. She couldn't fool him, nor could she fool herself. She wanted him as badly as he wanted her. It was crazy, outrageous, wonderful.

"Don't look at me like that," Chase said with a groan.

She gave herself a mental shake. "Like what?"

"Like you can't wait a minute longer."

She lowered her eyes, embarrassed. "I don't think I can."

He swore under his breath, stood abruptly and slapped some bills down on the table. "Come on," he said, "let's get out of here."

"We came on the tour bus, remember?"

"We'll get a taxi back."

"Chase —" she laughed "— that'll cost a fortune."

"I don't care what it costs. If we don't leave now we could be arrested. There are laws against people doing in public what I intend to do with you."

Lesley was sure her face turned five shades of red as they hurried out of Butchart Gardens. They located a taxi, and the second after Chase gave the driver the name of their hotel, he pulled her into his arms. His kiss was wet and wild and thorough. Thorough enough to hold them until they got back to the hotel.

Chase paid the driver and they raced hand in hand into the hotel and through the lobby, not stopping until they reached their room.

Chase's fingers shook when he inserted the key and Lesley's heart was touched by his eagerness.

"This is the most insane thing I've ever done in my life," she said, trying not to laugh.

The door swung open and Chase

drew her inside, closing the door and backing her against it.

"I was going to go berserk if I couldn't touch you the way I wanted," he whispered, kissing her with a hunger that echoed her own.

"Chase . . ." She wasn't sure what she wanted, only *that* she wanted.

Apparently he knew, because he scooped her into his arms and carried her to the bed.

An hour later, Lesley smiled to herself and buried her face in her husband's neck. With Chase she'd never be alone again. With Chase she felt whole, complete. Was this an illusion? She wasn't sure.

But right now she needed the feel of him, needed the reality of this man, this moment. She pressed her hands to his face and with tears she couldn't explain blurring her vision, she looked up at him.

"Thank you," she whispered.

He kissed her, his touch gentle.

"What's happening to us?" she asked, thinking he could help her understand.

"What do you mean?"

"Is this just good sex or is it more?"

"More," was his immediate response.

"Do I love you?" It obviously wasn't the question he'd expected her to ask, which was fine since it astonished even her.

"I don't know."

"Are you in love with me?"

His brow creased as if that required serious consideration. "I know I've never felt like this about any woman. What's happening between us, this physical thing, is as much of a surprise to me as it is you." He leaned forward and kissed the tip of her nose.

"I'm glad you decided to marry me," Chase continued, "although if this goes on much longer, I may be dead within a year."

Lesley laughed and, wrapping her arms around his neck, lifted her head just enough to kiss him.

"You're pure magic," he whispered against her lips.

"Me?"

He grinned.

She answered him with a grin of her own. "I don't know about you, but I'm starving."

Chase nuzzled her nose with his. "Let's not take any chances this time and order room service. It's ridiculous to pay for meals I never have a chance to eat."

After a leisurely lunch, they played tourist for the rest of the day, but didn't wander far from the hotel. They'd learned their lesson. They had high tea at the Empress Hotel, toured the museum, explored the undersea gardens.

They crammed as much as they could into the afternoon and returned, exhausted, to their hotel early that evening.

"Where do you want to go for dinner?" Chase asked.

"Dinner?" Lesley repeated. "I'm still full from lunch. And tea."

"Okay, then, what do you want to do?"

"Soak in a long, hot bath and take a nap. You kept me up half the night, remember?"

"A bath?" His eyes widened. "Really?"

Despite her exhaustion, Lesley smiled. "Later," she said and kissed him sweetly. "Give me an hour or two to regroup, okay?"

His face fell in mock disappointment.

"Come on," she said, holding her hand out to him. "You can nap with me, if you promise to sleep." She yawned loudly and pulled back the covers. The bath would come later. Right now it would only bring temptation for them both.

"I hoped we'd be in bed by five o'clock," Chase muttered, "but I never thought it would be to sleep. Some honeymoon this is turning out to be."

"Some honeymoon," Lesley agreed, smiling. She laid her head against the thick feather pillow and closed her eyes. Within seconds she could feel herself drift off.

The phone beside the bed rang, startling her badly. Before she could assimilate what was happening, Chase grabbed the receiver.

"Hello," he answered gruffly. Whoever was calling made him laugh. He placed his hand over the mouthpiece as he handed Lesley the phone. "It's Daisy."

"Daisy?" Lesley said, surprised to hear from her neighbor. "Hi."

"Trust me, I wouldn't be calling you at the hotel if it wasn't necessary."

"Don't worry. You weren't interrupting anything."

"Wanna bet?" Chase said loudly enough to be heard at the other end.

"Listen, Lesley, this isn't my idea of a fun call, but I figured you'd better know. Tony's been pestering me for information about you and Chase."

Lesley sat up in bed. "You didn't tell him anything, did you?"

"No, but the movers arrived while he was here and I saw him talking to the driver. He might've been able to get information out of him."

"I doubt it," she said, gnawing on her lower lip. "Those men are professionals. They know better than to give out information about their clients."

"That segment about you and Chase on television tonight didn't help. Tony phoned two seconds after the piece aired."

Lesley groaned. She'd forgotten

about that.

"What's wrong?" Chase asked.

"Nothing," she whispered.

"Daisy didn't call for no reason," he argued.

"I'll explain later," she said, although it wasn't a task she relished.

"It's Tony, isn't it?"

"Chase, please."

"All right, all right," he grumbled, but he wasn't happy and didn't bother to disguise it. He climbed out of bed and reached for his clothes, dressing with an urgency she didn't understand.

"Okay, I'm back," she told Daisy.

"Tony's looking to make trouble."

"I guess I shouldn't be surprised."

"I don't know why I'm so worried," Daisy muttered. "It isn't like he could do anything. You're already married."

"Well, what do you think he's going to do?"

She noticed Daisy's hesitation. "I don't know, but I wanted to warn you."

"Thanks," Lesley said, genuinely grateful. Tony seemed light-years away. Only a couple of days earlier she'd been convinced she loved him. That wasn't true anymore. Any feeling she still had was a memory, a ghost of the love she'd once felt.

"So?" Daisy said, her voice dipping suggestively. "How's the honeymoon?"

Lesley closed her eyes and sagged against the velvet headboard. "Wonderful."

"Are you two having fun with each other?"

"Daisy!"

"I meant sightseeing and all."

"I know *exactly* what you meant."

"Then why are you trying to be coy?"

"All right, if you must know, we're having a very good time. There — are you satisfied?"

"Hardly. I've got to tell you, Lesley, I could be jealous. It's been so long since I've been with a man, I feel like a virgin all over again."

Lesley laughed. "If Tony gives you any more trouble, let me know and I'll get a restraining order."

"You'd do that?" Daisy sounded relieved.

"In a heartbeat."

Chase stood on the other side of the room, his back to her. Lesley watched him for a moment and said to her neighbor, "Listen, we'll talk as soon as we get back."

"Which is when?"

"Day after tomorrow, but we'll be flying up to Alaska almost immediately. You have my cell number. Keep in touch, okay?"

"I will," Daisy promised and ended the conversation.

Lesley replaced the receiver. Her hand still on the phone, she mentally composed what she was going to say to Chase.

"So it *was* Tony," he commented, turning back to her.

"Yes. He's making a pest of himself." Chase's hands were in his pockets and he looked unsure. Of her and their marriage. It seemed a bit soon to be having doubts, and she said as much.

"He wants you."

"I know, but I married *you*." Her words didn't seem to reassure him. He stood there apparently deep in thought.

Kneeling on the bed, Lesley murmured, "I feel like having those chocolates and a hot bath. How about you?"

That got his attention. His eyes locked with hers and she started laughing. "Come here," she said, holding her arms out to Chase. "It's time you understood that neither of us has anything to fear from Tony. I've made my decision and chosen to be your wife. A jealous ex-fiancé doesn't stand a chance."

Chase remained where he was, as if he didn't quite believe her.

Lesley got up from the bed and was halfway across the room before she realized she was nearly naked. It didn't bother her — she was proud of her body. Chase had made her feel that way. She was focused on the man in front of her, not on herself.

Rising onto her toes, she kissed him lightly.

"Lesley . . ."

"Shhh."

He stood perfectly still, and with his eyes closed, allowed her to continue kissing him. When she was satisfied with his lips, she kissed the underside of his jaw, moving her mouth down his neck, then up to his ear. After what seemed like the longest moment of her life, he threaded his fingers through her hair and raised her face to his.

"I want you to be very sure."

"I am," she whispered. "I am sure."

He looked into her eyes. "A hot bath and chocolate sounds like an excellent suggestion," he said.

Lesley smiled contentedly. Marriage was far better than she'd ever imagined.

"Where are we going?" Lesley asked. They'd left Victoria that afternoon and had traveled down the Kitsap Peninsula, boarding the ferry from Bremerton to Seattle. Lesley had assumed they'd be heading directly back to her house. If so, Chase was taking an interesting route.

"There's something I want you to see."

She glanced at her watch and swallowed her impatience. They'd gotten a later start than they'd expected. Their morning had begun with a hot bath. At least the water had initially been hot, but by the time they finished, it had cooled considerably. Because their schedule was off, they'd been forced to wait for a later ferry.

Their flight to Alaska was leaving early the next morning, and Lesley had a hundred details she needed to take care of before then.

"There," Chase said, pulling into an asphalt parking lot.

"Where?" She didn't see anything.

"The billboard," he said.

Looking up, she saw the original billboard Chase had used to advertise for a wife. The sign had been changed and now read, in huge black letters, THANK YOU, LESLEY, FOR SHARING MY LIFE.

"Well?" he asked, waiting for her to

respond.

"I . . . Oh, Chase, that's so sweet and so romantic. I think I'm going to cry." She was struggling to hold back the tears.

"I want to make you happy, Lesley, for the rest of our lives." He brought her into his arms and kissed her.

Happiness frightened her. Every time she was truly content, truly at peace, something would go wrong, her happiness ruined. The first time it happened, she was a child. A six-year-old. She'd never been happier than the week before they were supposed to leave for Disneyland. Not only had the trip been canceled, but she'd lost her father.

She'd been excited about her wedding to Tony, planning the event, shopping for her wedding dress, choosing her clothes. But he'd broken their engagement, plunging her into depression and then numbness.

Lesley was happy now, and she couldn't help wondering what it would cost her this time.

TEN

Lesley's hand reached for Chase's as the airplane circled Fairbanks, Alaska, before descending. She'd found the view of Alaska's Mount McKinley, in Denali National Park, awe-inspiring. After living in Seattle, between the Cascade and Olympic mountain ranges, she thought being impressed by Denali was saying something. The tallest peak in North America rose from the land far below, crowned by a halo of clouds.

"Is it *all* so beautiful?" she asked as the plane made its final approach.

"There's beauty in every part of Alaska," Chase told her, "but some of it's more difficult to see. More subtle."

"I'm going to love Twin Creeks," she said, knowing it would be impossible not to, if the area was anything like the landscape she'd seen from the plane.

Chase's fingers tightened around hers. "I hope you do."

They landed and were met by a tall, burly man with a beard so thick it hid most of his face. Beneath his wool cap, she caught a glimpse of twinkling blue eyes.

"Pete Stone," Chase said casually, placing his arm around Lesley's shoulders. "This is Lesley."

"You done it? You actually done it?" Pete asked, briefly removing his wool cap and scratching his head. His hair was shoulder-length and as thick as his beard. "You got yourself a wife?"

"How do you do?" Lesley said formally, holding out her hand. "I'm Lesley Goodman." Pete ignored her proffered hand and reached for her instead, hauling her against him and hugging her so tightly, he lifted her three feet off the ground. Lesley wasn't offended so much as surprised. She cast a pleading glance at her husband, who didn't look any too pleased with this unexpected turn of events.

"Pete," Chase said stiffly. "Put her down. Lesley's not accustomed to being manhandled."

"You jealous?" Pete said, slowly releasing her. His grin would've been impossible to see beneath the mask of his beard, but his eyes sparkled with delight. "That tells me you care about this little slip of a girl."

Being nearly six feet tall, Lesley didn't think of herself as a little slip of anything. She couldn't help liking Pete despite his bear-hugging enthusiasm.

"Of course I care about her. I married her, didn't I?"

"You sure did, but then you said you was coming back with a wife if you had to marry yourself up with a polecat."

"Lesley's no polecat."

"I got eyes in my head," Pete said. "I can see that for myself."

"Good. Now, is the plane ready or not?" Chase asked, picking up two of their suitcases. He didn't look at Lesley and she sensed that Chase was annoyed by Pete's remark about his determination to find a wife. She hadn't accepted his proposal under any misconception. If she'd turned him down, he would've found someone else. She'd known that from the first.

Pete grabbed the two additional pieces of luggage and winked at Lesley. "The plane's been ready since yesterday. I flew down a day early and raised some heck."

"Okay, okay," Chase muttered. He turned to Lesley. "Do you mind leaving right away?" he asked as they approached the four-passenger plane.

"No," she assured him with a smile. She was eager to reach her new home, and she knew Chase was just as eager to get back. It would've been nice to spend some time in Fairbanks, but they'd have plenty of opportunity for that later.

"So," Pete said to Chase after they'd boarded the plane, "are you going to tell me how you did it?" The two men occupied the front seats, with Chase as the pilot, while Lesley sat in the back.

"Did what?"

"Got someone as beautiful as Lesley to marry you."

Chase was preoccupied, flipping a series of switches. "I asked her."

Lesley was mildly insulted that he'd condensed the story of their courtship into a simple three-word sentence.

"That was all it took?" Pete seemed astounded. He twisted around and looked at Lesley. "You got any single friends?"

"Daisy," she answered automatically, already missing her neighbor.

"Daisy," Pete repeated as if the sound of her name conjured up the image of a movie star. "I bet she's beautiful."

"She's divorced with two boys," Chase said, "and she recently started dating a guy she works with, so don't get your mind set on her."

Pete was quiet for a few minutes; silence was a rare commodity with this man, Lesley suspected. "I figured you'd get yourself a woman with a couple kids, liking the little rascals the way you do," he told Chase.

"Lesley suits me just fine." Chase reached for the small hand mike and spoke with the air traffic controller, awaiting his instructions. Within minutes they were in the air.

Chase hadn't told her he was a pilot; Lesley was impressed but not surprised. There was something so capable about him. So skilled and confident. She guessed that he was the kind of man who'd be equal to any challenge, who could solve any problem. Maybe that was typical of Alaskans.

"Won't it be dark by the time we arrive?" she asked.

Pete laughed as if she'd told a good joke.

"The sun's out until midnight this time of year," Chase explained. "Remember?"

Pete twisted around again. "Did Chase tell you much about Twin Creeks?"

"A little." Very little, she realized with a start. All she knew was that

Twin Creeks was near the pipeline and that Chase was employed by one of the major oil companies. The town was small, but there weren't any exceptionally large cities in Alaska. The population of Fairbanks, according to some information she'd read on the plane, was less than forty thousand.

"You tell her about the mosquitoes?" Pete asked Chase, his voice low and conspiratorial.

"Mosquitoes?" Lesley repeated. She'd considered them more of a tropical pest. There were plenty in the Seattle area, but the air was moist and vegetation abundant. She'd never thought there'd be mosquitoes in the Arctic.

"Mosquitoes are the Alaska state bird," Pete teased, smiling broadly.

"You ain't never seen 'em as big as we get 'em. But don't worry, they only stick around in June and July. Otherwise they leave us be."

"I have plenty of repellant at the cabin," Chase assured her, frowning.

"Twin Creeks is near the Gates of the Arctic wilderness park. Chase told you that, didn't he?"

Lesley couldn't remember if he had or not.

"We're at the base of the Brooks range, which is part of the Endicott mountains."

"How long does it take to drive to Fairbanks?" she asked.

"I don't know," Pete admitted, rubbing his beard as he considered her question. "I've always flown. We don't have a road that's open year-round, so not many folks drive that way. Mostly we fly. Folks in Twin Creeks mainly rely on planes for transportation. It's easier that way."

"I . . . see." Lesley was beginning to do just that. Twin Creeks wasn't a thriving community as she'd originally assumed. It was a station town with probably a handful of people. All right, she could live with that. She could adjust her thinking.

"Twin Creeks is on the edge of the Arctic wilderness," Chase said absently, responding to Pete's earlier remark about the town's location.

It was difficult to read his tone, but Lesley heard something she hadn't before. A hesitation, a reluctance, as if he feared that once she learned the truth about living in Alaska, she'd regret having married him. But she didn't. It wasn't possible, not anymore. Their honeymoon had seen to that.

"What about the wildlife?" she asked, curious now.

"We got everything you can imagine," Pete answered enthusiastically. "There's caribou, Dall sheep, bears —"

"Bears?" She refused to listen beyond that.

"They're a nuisance if you ask me," Pete continued. "That's why most of us have caches so —"

"What's a cache?" Lesley interrupted.

"A cache," he repeated as if he was sure she must know.

"It's like a small log cabin built on stilts," Chase explained. "It's spelled *c-a-c-h-e*, but pronounced cash."

"Bears and the like can't climb ladders," Pete added. "But they do climb poles, so we wrap tin around the beams to keep 'em off."

"What do you store there that the bears find so attractive?"

"It's a primitive freezer for meat in the winter."

"I keep extra fuel and bedding in mine," Pete said. "And anything else I don't want the wildlife gettin'. You've got to be careful what you put outside your door, but Chase will tell you all about that, so don't worry. We haven't lost anyone to bears in two, three years now." He laughed, and Lesley didn't know if he was teasing or not.

She swallowed uncomfortably and pushed the thought out of her mind. "I think moose are interesting creatures," she said conversationally, remembering Lori's comment.

"We get 'em every now and then, but not often." Once more it was Pete who answered.

By the time they landed, ninety minutes later, Lesley was both exhausted and worried. After they'd parked the plane in a hangar and unloaded their luggage, Pete drove them to a cabin nestled in a valley of alder, willow and birch trees. Lesley didn't see any other cabins along the way, but then she wasn't expecting Chase to live on a suburban street. Neighbors would have been welcome, but he didn't seem to have any within walking distance.

"See you in the morning," Pete said, delivering two of the suitcases to the porch. He left immediately, after slapping Chase on the back and making a comment Lesley couldn't hear. She figured Pete was issuing some unsolicited marital advice.

"You're meeting him in the morning?" Lesley asked. Chase had told her he needed to be back at work. But she'd assumed he wouldn't have to go in right away, that he'd be able to recover from his travels first.

"He's picking me up," Chase said. "I have to check in. I won't stay long, I promise." They were standing on the porch and Lesley was eager to get a look at her new home. The outside didn't really tell her much. She'd seen vacation homes that were larger than this.

Chase unlocked the door and turned to her, sweeping her off her feet as if she weighed no more than the suitcase. His actions took her by surprise and she gasped with pleasure when she realized he was following tradition by carrying her over the threshold.

Lesley closed her eyes and reveled in the splendor of being in his arms. They kissed briefly, then Chase carried her into the bedroom and they sat on the edge of the bed together.

"This has been the longest day of my life," Lesley said with a yawn. "I could kill for a hot bath and room service, but I don't think I'd stay awake long enough for either."

"I've dreamed of having you in this bed with me," he said in a low voice.

Lesley cupped his face and tenderly kissed his lips. "Come on. I'll help you bring in the luggage."

"Nonsense," Chase countered. "It's no problem. I'll get it."

Lesley didn't object. While Chase dealt with their suitcases, she could explore their home. The bedroom was cozy and masculine-looking. The walls were made of a light wood — pine, she guessed — with a double closet that had two drawers below each door.

A picture was the only thing on the dresser and Lesley knew in an instant that the couple staring back at her from the brass frame were Chase's parents. The bed was large, too big for the room, but that didn't bother her. The floor was wood, too, with several thick, braided throw rugs.

There was a small guest room across the hall, simply furnished with an iron bedstead and a chest of draw-ers.

Moving into the living room, Lesley

admired the huge rock fireplace. It took up nearly all of one wall. He had a television, DVD player and music system. She'd known there was electricity; she'd made a point of asking.

The furniture was homey and inviting. A recliner and an overstuffed sofa, plus a rocking chair. Chase loved books, if the overflowing bookcases were any indication. Between two of them stood a rough-hewn desk that held a laptop computer.

A microwave caught her eye from the kitchen counter, which was a faded red linoleum, and she moved in that direction. The huge refrigerator and freezer stood side by side and looked new, dominating one wall. Everything else, including the dishwasher and stove, were ancient-looking. She'd make the best of it,

Lesley decided, but she was putting her word in early. The kitchen was often the heart of a home and she intended to make theirs as modern and comfortable as possible. From the looks of it, she had her work cut out for her.

"Well?" Chase asked from behind her. "What do you think?"

"I think," she said, turning and hugging him around the middle, "that I could get used to living here with you."

Chase sighed as if she'd just removed a giant weight from his shoulders. "Good. I realized as soon as I saw Pete that I hadn't really prepared you for Twin Creeks. It's not what you'd call a thriving metropolis."

"I've noticed. Are there neighbors?"

"Some," he answered cryptically.

He held her close, and she couldn't read his expression.

"Nearby?"

"Not exactly. So, are you ready for bed?" he asked, changing the subject, but not smoothly enough for her not to notice.

"I've decided I'll have a bath, after all." She planned to soak out the stiffness of all those hours cooped up inside planes.

"There's one problem," he said, sounding chagrined. "I don't have a tub."

Lesley stared at him. "Pardon?"

"There's only a shower. It's all I've ever needed. At some point we can install a bathtub, if you want."

"Okay. I'll manage." A shower instead of a bath was a minor inconvenience. She'd adjust.

Chase needed to make a couple of calls and while he was busy, Lesley showered and readied for bed. Her husband of four days undressed, showered and climbed into bed with her.

The sheets were cold and instinctively Lesley nestled close to Chase. He brought her into the warm alcove of his arms, gently kissing her hair.

"Good night," Lesley whispered when he turned off the light.

" 'Night." The light was off, but the room was still bright. She'd adjust to sunlight in the middle of the night, too, Lesley reasoned. But it now seemed that she was going to have to make more adjustments than she'd realized.

She rolled onto her side and positioned the pillow to cradle her head.

She was too tired to care, too tired to do anything but sleep.

Chase, however, had other ideas. . . .

Lesley smiled softly to herself as he whispered in her ear.

"You know what I want."

"Yes." She slipped onto her back and lifted her arms to him in welcome. She *did* know what he wanted. And tired or not, she wanted the same thing.

Chase was awakened by the alarm. His eyes burned and he felt as if he were fighting his way out of a fog before he realized what he needed to do to end the irritating noise.

Lesley didn't so much as stir. He was pleased that the buzzer hadn't woken her. He'd like nothing better than to stay in bed and wake his wife and linger there with her.

That wasn't possible, though. Not this morning. There'd be plenty of other mornings when they could. He looked forward to those times with pleasure.

Chase slipped out of bed and reached for his jeans and shirt. Wandering into the bathroom, he splashed cold water onto his face in a desperate effort to wake up. He'd report in to work, do what needed to be done and leave again. It shouldn't take more than thirty minutes, an hour at the most. There was a chance he'd be home before Lesley even woke up.

He smiled the whole time he made himself a cup of coffee. He sat in the recliner and laced his boots, put on a light jacket and let himself out the door.

Pete was just pulling into his yard when Chase walked down the two front steps. He sipped from his coffee in its travel mug and walked toward his friend.

"Trouble," Pete greeted him.

"What's going on?"

"Don't know."

"It isn't going to take long, is it?" Chase knew the answer to that already. Nothing was ever easy around the pump station.

"I gotta tell you," Pete said to him good-naturedly, "your arrival back couldn't have been more timely."

Chase released a four-letter word beneath his breath. He'd wait an hour or so, call Lesley and explain. This certainly wasn't the way he wanted their lives together to begin, but it couldn't be helped. Too bad she'd learn the truth so soon.

Lesley woke to blazing sunshine. That was how she'd gone to sleep, too. She turned her head toward Chase, surprised to find the other half of the bed empty. Swallowing her disappointment, she tossed aside the covers and sat on the edge of the mattress.

Chase had parked their suitcases by the bedroom door. Lesley decided to unpack first, and by the time she was through, she hoped Chase would be back.

She dressed, then looked in the cupboard for something to eat. As soon as Chase returned, they'd need to do some grocery shopping. Since he'd been gone for several weeks, they needed to restock the essentials.

The phone rang while she was munching on dry cereal.

"Hello," she answered enthusiastically, knowing it was likely to be Chase; she was right.

"Lesley, I've run into some problems here at the station."

"Will you be long?"

"I don't know. Do you think you can manage without me for a while?"

"Of course."

"I can send Pete if you'd rather not be alone."

"I'll be fine, and I certainly don't need a babysitter."

He hesitated. "Don't go wandering off by yourself, all right?"

"Don't worry. With bears and wolves roaming around, I won't be taking any strolls."

"I'm sorry about this," he said re-gretfully.

"I'll be fine."

"You're sure?"

"Chase, stop worrying, I'm a big girl."

"I've got to go."

"I know. Just answer one thing. We need groceries. Would you mind if I took your truck and drove into town and picked up a few items?" She eyed her bowl of cereal. "We need milk, eggs and so on."

She heard him curse under his breath. "Groceries. I didn't think of that. Hold off, would you, for a little while? I'll be back as soon as I can."

"I know." She was lonely for him already, but determined to be a help-mate and not a problem.

Another hour passed and she'd completely reorganized their bedroom. She consolidated the things in Chase's dresser to make room for hers and hung what she could in his cramped closet. When Chase had a few minutes to spare, she needed him to weed out anything he didn't need.

The sound of an approaching car was a welcome distraction. Hoping it was Chase, she hurried onto the front porch — to see Pete driving toward the house in his four-wheel-drive vehicle.

"Howdy," he called, waving as he climbed out of the truck. "Chase sent me to check up on you."

"I'm fine. Really."

"He had me pick up a few things on the way." He reached inside the cab and lifted out two bags of groceries and carried them into the house.

"I could've gone myself." She was disappointed that Chase didn't trust her enough to find her way around. Just how lost could she get?

"Chase wanted to introduce you around town himself," Pete explained. He seemed to have read her thoughts. He set the bags on the kitchen counter and Lesley investigated their contents. For a bachelor, Pete had done a good job.

"What do I owe you?" she asked.

"Nothing," Chase's friend responded, helping himself to a cup of coffee. "Chase took care of it. He's got an account at the store and they bill him monthly."

"How . . . quaint."

Pete added two teaspoons of sugar, stirring vigorously. "Chase said you like to cook."

"I do," she responded. Since he didn't show any signs of leaving, she poured herself a cup of coffee and joined him at the kitchen table.

"There's plenty of deer meat in the freezer."

"Deer?"

"You never cooked deer before? What about caribou?"

"Neither one." Didn't anyone dine on good old-fashioned beef in Alaska?

"Don't worry. It cooks up like beef and doesn't taste all that different. You'll be fine."

Lesley appreciated his confidence even if she didn't share it.

"So," Pete said, relaxing in his chair, hands encircling the mug, "what do you think of the cabin?"

Lesley wasn't sure how to answer.

It was certainly livable, but nothing like she'd expected. However, as she'd said to herself countless times, she'd adjust. "It's homey," she said, trying to be diplomatic about it.

"Chase bought it 'specially for you."

Lesley lowered her eyes. That couldn't possibly be true. He hadn't known her long enough to have chosen this cabin for her.

"He's only been living here a few months," Pete went on. "He decided back in March that he wasn't going through another winter without a wife, so he started getting ready for one. The first thing he did was buy this place and move off the station."

"Do you live at the station?"

"Nope. I bought myself a cabin, too, year or so ago.

"Chase has lots of plans to remodel,

but he wanted to wait until he found the right woman so they could plan the changes together."

Lesley looked around, the ideas already beginning to form. If they knocked out the wall between the living room and kitchen, they could get rid of the cramped feeling.

"Chase did all right for himself," Pete said, sounding proud of his friend. "I gotta tell you, I laughed when he told me he was going to Seattle and bringing himself back a wife."

"Why didn't he marry someone from around here?" Lesley asked. She already knew the answer but wanted to see what he'd say.

"First off, there aren't any available women in Twin Creeks. He might've met a woman in Fairbanks — used to go out with a couple different ones — but he figured his chances were better in Seattle. And he was right!"

"I'm glad he did go to Seattle."

"He seems pleased about it. This is the first time I've seen Chase smile in a year, ever since his father died. He took it hard, you know."

Lesley pretended she did. Although she'd told him about her own parents, Chase hadn't said much about his, just that they were both dead.

"So soon after his mother — that darn near killed him. He's all alone now, no brothers or sisters, and he needed someone to belong to the way we all do. I don't know that he's ever said that, but it's the reason he was so keen on marryin'."

"What about you?" Lesley asked. "Why haven't you married?"

"I did once, about ten years back, but it didn't work out." Pain flickered in his eyes. "Pamela didn't last the winter. I hope for Chase's sake you're different. He's already crazy about you, and if you left him, it'd probably break his heart."

"I'm not leaving." It would take a lot more than a harsh winter to change her mind about her commitment to Chase. She'd never taken duty lightly and she'd pledged before her friends and God to stand by Chase as his wife, his lover, his partner.

"Good." Pete's twinkling blue eyes were back.

"Chase sent you out to babysit me, didn't he?"

Pete laughed. "Not exactly. He was a little afraid you were gonna get curious and do some exploring."

"Not after the conversation we had about the bears." Lesley shuddered dramatically.

"They aren't gonna hurt you. You leave 'em alone and they'll leave you alone. You might want to ask Chase to take you to the dump and that way you'll get to see 'em firsthand."

"They hang around the dump?"

"Sure do, sorting through the garbage lookin' for goodies. We've tried plenty of ways to keep 'em away, but nothing seems to work and we finally gave up."

"I see." Lesley wasn't impressed. "Has anyone thought to bury the garbage?" The solution seemed simple to her.

"Obviously you've never tried to dig tundra. It's like cement an inch below

379

the surface."

"What's wrong at the station?" Lesley asked, looking at her watch. It was well past noon.

"Can't rightly say, but whatever it is will have to be fixed before Chase can come home. Trust me, he isn't any happier about this than you. Chase isn't normally a swearing man, but he was cursin' a blue streak this morning. He'll give you a call the minute he can."

"I'd like to see the town," Lesley said. She was eager to meet the other women and become a part of the community. It was too late in the year to apply for a full-time teaching position, but she could make arrangements to get her certificate and sign up as a substitute.

"Chase will take you around himself," Pete said again. "It wouldn't be right for me to be introducin' you."

"I know." She sighed. "Tell me about Twin Creeks, would you?"

"Ah . . . there's not much to tell."

"What about stores?"

He shrugged. "We order most everything through the catalog and on the Internet."

"There's a grocery store."

"Oh, sure, but it's small."

Well, she wasn't expecting one with a deli and valet parking.

"What's the population of Twin Creeks?"

Pete wasn't one who could easily disguise his feelings, and she could see from the way his eyes darted past hers that he'd prefer to avoid answering. "We've had, uh, something of a population boom since the last census."

"What's the official total?"

"You might want to talk to Chase about that."

"I'm asking *you*," she pressed, growing impatient. "A thousand?"

"Less 'n that," he said, drinking what remained of his coffee.

"How many less?"

"A, uh, few hundred less."

"All right, five hundred people, then?"

"No . . ."

Lesley pinched her lips together. "Just tell me. I hate guessing games."

"Forty," Pete mumbled into the empty mug.

"Adults?" Her heart felt as if it'd stopped.

"No, that's counting everyone, including Mrs. Davis's cat."

Eleven

"How many women live in Twin Creeks?" Lesley demanded.

"Including you?" Pete asked, looking decidedly uncomfortable by this time. He clutched his coffee mug with both hands and sat staring into it, as though he expected the answer to appear there.

"Of course I mean including me!"

"That makes a grand total of five then." He continued to hold on to his mug as if it were the Holy Grail.

"You mean to tell me there're only *five* women in the entire town?"

"Five women within five hundred miles, I suspect, when you get right down to it." If his face got much closer to the mug, his nose would disappear inside it.

"Tell me about the other women," Lesley insisted. She was pacing in her agitation. Chase had purposely withheld this information about Twin Creeks from her. Fool that she was, she hadn't even thought to ask, assuming that when he mentioned the town there actually *was* one!

"There's Thelma Davis," Pete said enthusiastically. "She's married to Milton and they're both in their sixties. Thelma runs the grocery store and she loves to gossip. You'll get along with her just fine. Gladys Thornton might be kind of a problem, though. She's a little crabby and not the sociable sort, so most folks just leave her be."

"Is there anyone close to my age?"

"Heather's twelve," Pete replied, looking up for the first time. "She lives with Thelma Davis. I never did understand the connection. Heather isn't her granddaughter, but they're related in some way."

The woman closest to her in age was a twelve-year-old girl! Lesley's heart plummeted.

"You'll like Margaret, though. She's a real social butterfly. The minute she hears Chase brought himself back a wife, she'll be by to introduce herself."

"How old is Margaret?"

"Darned if I know. In her fifties, I guess. She doesn't like to discuss her age and tries to pretend she's younger."

"I . . . see."

"I'd best be heading back," Pete said, obviously eager to leave. "I know it's a lot to ask, but would you mind not tellin' Chase that I was the one who told you? We've been friends for a long time and I'd hate for him to take this personally. Me spillin' the beans to you, I mean."

"I'm not making any promises."

Pete left as if he couldn't get away fast enough.

An hour later, Lesley still hadn't decided what to do, if anything. Chase had misled her, true enough, but she wasn't convinced it mattered. She probably would've married him anyway.

No wonder he'd been so interested in Seattle's history and the Mercer brides. Although more than a hundred years had passed since that time, she was doing basically the same thing as those women, moving to a frontier wilderness and marrying a man she barely knew.

Chase arrived shortly after one o'clock, looking discouraged. Lesley met him at the front door and waited, wondering what to say.

Without a word of greeting, Chase pulled her into his arms and his mouth came down on hers. The familiar taste of him offered comfort and reassurance.

"I missed you," he whispered into her hair, his arms wrapped around her waist.

"I missed you, too."

"Pete brought the groceries? Did he get enough of everything?"

Lesley nodded. "Plenty." She broke away from him. "I didn't know your parents died so recently," she said. She slipped her arm around him and led him into the kitchen. He had to be hungry so she opened a can of chili and began heating that for him. Keeping her hands occupied helped; she didn't want him to guess how much Pete's information had disturbed her.

Chase stood with his back against the counter. "My mom passed away less than two years ago. She died of a heart attack. It was sudden and so much of a shock that my father followed last year. They say people don't die of broken hearts, but I swear that isn't true. My dad was lost without Mom, and I believe he willed himself to die."

"I'm sorry, Chase, I didn't know."

"I meant to tell you."

"It was after their deaths that you decided to marry?"

"Yes," he admitted, watching her closely. "Does that upset you?"

"No." Her reasons for accepting his proposal hadn't been exactly flawless. She'd been escaping her love for Tony, running because she feared she was too weak to withstand her attraction to him. Recently those reasons had blurred in her mind, thanks to her doubts and the unexpected happiness she'd found with Chase. They'd bonded much sooner than she'd anticipated. They belonged together now and if it was Tony's craziness that had brought them to this point, that didn't matter. What did was her life with Chase.

"How's everything at the station?" she asked, placing the steaming bowl of chili on the table and taking out a box of soda crackers.

"Not good. We're going to need a part." He wiped his face with one hand, ignoring the lunch she'd prepared for him. "I hate doing this to you so soon, but it looks like I'll have to go after the motor myself."

"You're *leaving?*" She felt as though she'd been punched by the unexpectedness of it. "How long will you be gone?"

"I don't know yet. A day, possibly two."

It wasn't the end of the world, but she felt isolated and alone as it was. Without Chase she might as well be off floating on an iceberg.

"When do you have to go?" she asked.

"Soon. Listen, sweetheart, I don't want this any more than you do, but it can't be avoided."

Sweetheart. He'd never used affectionate terms with her before. He was genuinely worried, as well he should be. He was going to have to introduce her to the people of Twin Creeks sooner or later, and she knew he'd prefer to do that personally, rather than have her discover the truth on her own while he was away. Of course, he had no idea Pete had already "spilled the beans," as he'd put it.

"I'll pack an overnight bag for you," she offered, half waiting for him to stop her right then and explain.

"Lesley."

She smiled to herself, relieved at the hesitation she heard in his voice. He was going to tell her.

He moved behind her, wrapped his arms around her waist and slipped his hand inside her light sweater. "We won't be able to sleep together to-night."

"Yes, I know." Her voice sounded thick even to her own ears.

He caught her earlobe between his teeth. "One night can feel like a very long time," he said in a whisper.

"It won't be so bad."

"It could be, though."

"Oh." Brilliant conversation was beyond her when he touched her this way.

His lips nibbled at her ear and hot sensation spread though her. "I was thinking you might want to give me something to send me off."

"Like what?" Not that she didn't know *exactly* what he meant, but she was annoyed with him because he was so casual about letting her learn the truth.

"I was in a foul mood all morning," Chase continued, "hurrying because I wanted to get home." He laughed. "Wanting to rush home was a new experience."

"What was the big hurry?"

"Do you honestly need me to say?" He gave another throaty chuckle. "I can't get enough of you. We make love and instead of glorying in the satisfaction, I immediately start wondering when I can have you again. Have you put a spell on me?"

"No." If anything she was the one who'd been enchanted.

He groaned. "Pete will be here in five minutes."

She nodded, turning her head away.

"You're crying," he said with a frown. He held her face gently, brushing the hair from her brow, using his thumbs to wipe away the moisture on her cheeks.

She gazed up at him, blinking hard, hardly able to see him through her tears. Closing her eyes, she shook her head. "Go, or you'll be late."

"I'm not leaving until you tell me what's wrong."

"Pete's coming." She pushed him away.

"He'll wait. Lesley, tell me what's wrong." He reached for an overnight bag, stuffing it with the essentials he'd need as he waited for her response.

She didn't, couldn't, respond.

"You're upset because I have to leave you so soon," he said, "but, sweetheart, I told you. It can't be helped."

She was so furious by this time that she clenched her fists at her sides. "Pete told me his wife didn't last the winter. My sympathy was with Pete because of the weak woman he married. I was making all sorts of judgmental statements in my head, automatically blaming her. I blamed *her,* without the benefit of the doubt. I considered her weak and —"

"What does Pete's marriage have to do with us?" Chase took her by the arms, studying her intensely. A horn honked outside and he cast an irritated look over his shoulder.

"Go," she said again, freeing herself

from his hold. "Just go."

"I can't, Lesley, not with you feeling like this."

She swiped impatiently at her tears. "It might've helped if you'd let me know Twin Creeks is nothing more than . . . than a hole in the road. There are only five women here. Three of them are years older than I am, the fourth is a twelve-year-old girl and the other one is . . . me."

The honking went on longer and more urgently this time.

"Go on," she said, squaring her shoulders. "Pete's waiting."

Chase wavered, took one step toward the door, but then returned to her. "Will you be here when I get back?"

She had to think about that for a moment, then nodded.

He briefly closed his eyes. "Thank you for that." He left without kissing her. Without touching her. And without saying goodbye.

Lesley ended up throwing out the chili she'd prepared for Chase. She'd never been fond of it herself, although Chase certainly seemed to be if his cupboard was any indication. There was an entire shelf filled with nothing but cans of chili.

She moved from one room to the next, feeling sorry for herself. She'd let the opportunity to really talk about their situation slip through her fingers.

Her cheeks burned at the memory. They'd kissed — and then fought. But their physical longing for each other hadn't diminished.

Their relationship hadn't started out that way. This was a new development. One that had taken them both by storm.

Lesley delighted in how frequently Chase wanted her. Her joy was made complete by the ready response he evoked in her. But their mutual passion meant she not only needed him, she'd become dependent on him. This was the very thing she'd come to fear with Tony — this total giving of herself. Yet it was what she'd done with Chase. He ruled her head and her heart, as thoroughly as Tony once had. No, even more so.

Was this love? She didn't know. All she knew was that she couldn't be without her husband, but didn't want to lose herself in him.

Tucking her arms around her waist,

she wondered how she'd ever manage to fill up the time without Chase.

Chase impatiently filled out the registration forms at the Fairbanks hotel. The sooner he finished, the sooner he could call Lesley.

He wanted to kick himself. He'd known from the moment he arrived home that something was bothering her. He'd seen it in her eyes and in the way she preoccupied herself with making him lunch. He should have settled things between them right then.

Once he had the key to his room, he glanced longingly at the coffee shop. He hadn't eaten since breakfast and that had been a quick cup of coffee and a blueberry muffin.

He'd eat later, he decided, after

he'd spoken to Lesley, after he'd explained, if that was possible. He couldn't stand it if she left. She already meant too much to him.

He let himself into the stark hotel room and after dumping his overnight bag on the bed, sat on the edge of it and reached for the room phone. His hand was eager as he punched out the number.

She answered on the second ring.

"Lesley, hello." Now that he could talk to her, he didn't know what to say. The need to explain had burned in him the entire flight into Fairbanks, and now he was speechless.

"Chase?"

"I just got here."

"How are you? Did you have a good flight?"

"I suppose so. How are *you*?" He

needed to know that before he proceeded.

"Fine."

The way she said it told him she wasn't. "I realize it's probably not a good idea to have this conversation over the phone."

"We'll talk later," she said, but Chase was afraid that might be too late.

"I didn't want this misunderstanding to ruin what we have."

"And what *do* we have, Chase?" she asked, her voice a mere whisper.

"A marriage," he returned without hesitation. "A fledgling marriage, which means we need to learn to communicate with each other. I'm going to need help."

"We'll learn," she said, and there was a new strength in the words that reassured him.

"I'm sorry I didn't tell you more about Twin Creeks. There always seemed to be other things to discuss and . . . it didn't seem all that important."

Lesley had no comment.

Chase pressed his hand to his forehead. "That isn't true," he said in a voice so low, he wondered if she could hear him. "I was afraid that if you did know you'd change your mind about marrying me." He was taking one of the biggest risks of his life admitting it, but that was what made honesty of such high value. It was often expensive. But Lesley deserved nothing less.

"There'll never be a teaching position for me here, will there?"

"No." Once more the truth stabbed

at him.

"What did you expect me to do with my time?"

"Whatever you want. You can take correspondence courses, teach them if you'd like. Sometime you might want to start a business. The Internet's created a lot of possibilities. Whatever you choose will have my full emotional and monetary support. More than anything else, I want you to be happy."

"That all sounds good in theory, but I don't know how it'll work in practice."

"Time will show us." He felt as though he was fighting for his marriage. Either he convinced her here and now that he was serious or he'd lose her. Maybe not now but later, sometime down the road.

He couldn't bear to think of his life without her. It seemed impossible that she could own his heart after so short a time. "Give us a chance — that's all I'm asking."

"All right," she agreed in a whisper.

Chase scowled at the phone. He didn't know if what he'd said had made a difference or not. All he could do was hope that it had.

Chase had told her there was beauty in every part of Alaska but that some of it wasn't immediately obvious. The beauty around Twin Creeks was dark — that was how she'd describe it. Lesley stood outside his four-wheel-drive vehicle. She couldn't shake the feeling that life was very fragile in this part of the world.

The colors she saw thrilled her.

Wild splashes of vibrant orange, purple and red covered the grassy and lichened meadows. Pencil-thin waterfalls traced delicate vertical slopes, pooling into a clear lake. The valley wasn't like the rain forest of western Washington, but it was filled with life.

A moose grazed in the distance and she wondered if the great beast was plagued by mosquitoes the same way she'd been. Pete wasn't teasing when he'd warned her. These were the most irritating and persistent variety she'd ever encountered.

She'd found the keys to Chase's truck in a kitchen drawer. After less than twenty-four hours on her own, she was going stir-crazy. Chase had been adamant about not exploring on her own, but she didn't have much choice. If she had to stay inside the cabin one more minute, Lesley was convinced she'd go mad. Her books and other things hadn't arrived, and she didn't feel like emailing any of her friends. Not yet.

Anyway, it was time she introduced herself to the ladies of Twin Creeks, she'd decided, but she'd gotten sidetracked on her way into town.

The sight of the moose had captivated her and she'd parked on the side of the road to watch.

She'd soon become engrossed in the landscape. She lingered there, enjoying the beauty but aware of the dangers. After a while, she climbed back inside the truck and drove to town.

Twin Creeks itself didn't amount to much. She'd visited rest stops that were bigger than this town. She counted three buildings — a combination grocery store and gas station, a tavern and a tiny post office. There wasn't even a church.

The sidewalks, if she could call them that, were made of wooden boards that linked the three main structures. She saw a handful of houses in the distance.

Lesley parked and turned off the engine. A face peered out from behind the tattered curtains in the tavern. She pretended she hadn't noticed and got out of the truck, walking toward the grocery. If she remembered correctly, Thelma Davis ran the store.

"Hello," Lesley said to the middle-aged woman behind the counter, determined to be friendly. "I'm Lesley Goodman, Chase's wife."

"Thelma Davis."

Lesley glanced around. Thelma's business must be prospering. She not only carried food and cleaning supplies, but rented DVDs, sold yarn and other craft supplies, in addition to a smattering of just about everything else.

"Heard this morning that Chase got married," Thelma said, coming around the counter. "Welcome to Twin Creeks. Everyone around here is fond of Chase and we hope you'll be real happy."

"Thank you."

"Ever been to Alaska before? Don't answer that. I can see you haven't. You'll never be colder in your life, that much I can promise you. Some say this is really what hell will be like.

Personally, I don't intend on finding out."

"How long have you lived here?" Lesley asked.

Thelma squinted. "We were one of the first ones to move up this way when word came that the pipeline was going through. I was just a young married. That's, oh, more than forty years now. We love it, but the winters take some getting used to."

That Lesley could believe.

"We'll want to have a party for you two. I hope you don't mind us throwing a get-together in your honor. There isn't a lot of entertainment here, but we do our best to have fun."

"I love parties."

Thelma's hands rested on her hips. "We'll have it at our house, since we've got the biggest living room in town. Are you and Chase thinking of starting a family soon? It's been years since we had a baby born in Twin Creeks."

"Ah . . ." Lesley wasn't sure how to answer that.

"Forgive me, Lesley, I shouldn't be pressuring you about babies. It's just that we're so happy to have another woman, especially a young one."

"I'm pleased to meet you, too."

"If you have a minute I'll call Margaret and get Heather and we'll have coffee and talk. Do you have time for that? Everyone's dying to meet you, even Gladys. We're eager to do whatever we can to make you feel welcome."

"I'd love to meet everyone." The sooner the better. If Chase was going to be away often, her link with the others would be vital to her sanity.

"I knew I was going to like you." Thelma grinned. "The minute Pete mentioned Chase had brought back a wife and described you, I knew we'd be good friends. I think Pete's half smitten with you himself, which to my way of thinking is good. It's about time the men in this community thought about getting married and starting families. That's what Twin Creeks really needs."

Lesley couldn't agree more.

She stayed to meet the other women and by the time she left they'd talked for two hours. Rarely had Lesley been more impressed with anyone. They were like frontier women — resourceful, independent, with a strong sense of community. After the first half hour with the others, Lesley felt as if she'd known them all her life. The genuine warmth of her welcome was exactly what she needed. When she returned to the house, she felt excited to be part of this small but thriving community.

Lesley wasn't home more than five minutes when the phone rang. She answered it eagerly, thinking it would be Chase. There was so much she wanted to tell him.

"Hello."

"Lesley, it's your mother." Their conversations invariably started with June Campbell-Sterne announcing her parental status as if Lesley had forgotten.

"Mom?" She couldn't have been more shocked if Daisy had arrived on her doorstep.

"It's true then, isn't it? You're married and living with some crazy man in Alaska."

"Mom, it isn't as bad as it sounds." She should've tried phoning them again, had planned to, but she'd been too involved in becoming familiar with her new environment.

"When Tony contacted us —"

"Tony?" Lesley said, fuming. Daisy had warned her that her former fiancé was up to no good, but she'd never dreamed he'd resort to contacting her family to make trouble.

"Tony was kind enough to call us and let us know you'd gotten married, which is more than I can say for you."

"Trust me, Mom, Tony did *not* have my best interests at heart."

"I don't believe that."

"He's being jealous and spiteful."

Her mother breathed in deeply as if she was trying to control her temper. "Is it true that you married a man who advertised for a wife on a Seattle billboard?"

"Mom . . ."

"It is true?"

"Yes, but I didn't answer his ad, if that's what you're thinking. I know you're hurt," she said, trying to diffuse her mother's disappointment and anger, "and I apologize for not letting you know, but Chase only had a few days left in Seattle and you and Ken were traveling and I tried to call your cell and —"

"As it happened, we returned early, but you didn't know that because you just assumed we were gone. You're my only child. Didn't you stop to think that I'd want to be at your wedding?"

"Mom, I'm sorry."

"Tony says you don't even know the man you married. That you weren't in your right mind. He sounded very worried about you."

"None of that's true. I'm very happy with Chase."

"I won't believe that until I see you for myself and meet this man you've married. Ken's already made the flight arrangements for me. I'll be leaving first thing tomorrow morning and landing in Fairbanks at some horrible hour. I have no idea how to reach Twin Creeks from there, but I'll manage if I have to go by dogsled."

"I'll fly down and meet you in Fairbanks," Lesley said, thinking quickly. "Then we'll fly back to-

415

gether." She wanted Chase to meet her mother, but she would rather have waited until they'd settled into their lives together.

"All right." Some of the defensiveness was gone from her mother's voice.

"If you'd like to talk to someone about me and Chase, I suggest you contact Daisy instead of Tony."

"It broke my heart when you ended your engagement to Tony," her mother said.

"Mother, *he* married someone else! I didn't end the engagement — he did. Despite the claims he's making now."

"Look what's happened to you. Just look."

"Mother! I'm married to a wonderful man."

"As I said, I'll judge that for myself. See you tomorrow." She gave her arrival time and Lesley wrote it down on a pad by the phone. Now all she needed to do was find a way of reaching Fairbanks and meeting her mother's plane.

Chase clutched his cell phone so hard, he was afraid he might break it. "What do you mean she isn't at the house?" he demanded, scowling at Pete's unsatisfactory response. He'd spent the most frustrating day of his life, first having to deal with the motor company and then attempting to contact Lesley. He'd tried repeatedly that afternoon with no answer.

There were any number of reasons she might not have answered the phone, but he'd started to worry. Two hours of no response, and he was beside himself. He'd called Pete and had his friend drive over and check out the cabin for himself.

"The door was locked," Pete explained, "so I couldn't get inside. What did she lock it for?"

"Lesley's from the city — they lock everything there," Chase said, trying to figure out where she could've gone.

"When she heard how small Twin Creeks was, she seemed upset," Pete said, sounding guilty.

"We already settled that," Chase said irritably. "Where could she be?" The dangers she could encounter raced through his mind. "Do you think she might have wandered away from the cabin?"

"No."

Chase stiffened. "What makes you so certain?"

"The truck's gone."

"The truck! Well, why didn't you say so earlier?"

He felt Pete's hesitation. "There's something you're not telling me."

"Chase, you're my best friend. I don't want to be the one to tell you your wife walked out on you."

"*What?* She left?" The constriction in his chest produced a sharp pain. "She drove?" His heart did a wild tumble as he calculated how long it would take him to rent a car and catch up with her.

"No," Pete said, "she went out to the field and parked the car there. She paid Jim Perkins to fly her into Fairbanks."

"Without a word to anyone, she

just . . . up and left?"

"I'm sorry, Chase, I really am."

"What time will she be landing?"

"Not sure. All I know is what I heard from Johnny at the field. He only heard part of the conversation. What are you gonna do?"

"I don't know yet." Chase was in shock. His wife of less than a week had deserted him.

"You aren't gonna let her go, are you?"

"No." He'd find Lesley, somehow, someway, and convince her to give their marriage another chance.

TWELVE

"Mom." Lesley ran forward and hugged her mother as June Campbell-Sterne entered the arrivals lounge. Unexpected tears sprang to Lesley's eyes and she blinked them back, surprised by the emotion.

The tears were most likely due to the restless night she'd spent in a hotel close to the airport. Apparently Chase hadn't returned to Twin Creeks the way he'd assumed, otherwise he would've seen her message or answered her calls. She'd tried the home phone *and* his cell, with no results. He must be someplace here in Fairbanks. Unfortunately Lesley hadn't asked him for the name of his hotel, since he'd originally planned to be in town only one night.

It seemed ridiculous to contact every hotel in town and ask for Chase. She'd probably be back in Twin Creeks before her husband.

"Let me get a good look at you," June insisted, taking a step back while holding Lesley's shoulders. Her mother had tears in her eyes, as well. "Oh, sweetie, how are you?"

"I feel wonderful. See! Married life agrees with me." She slipped an arm around her mother's waist and together they strolled toward the luggage carousels.

"I'll admit to being curious about your husband. Honestly, Lesley, what kind of man advertises for a wife?"

Lesley laughed, remembering that her own response had been similar. "He's not crazy — just resourceful."

"I don't mind telling you, this whole thing has both Ken and me concerned. It just isn't like you to marry a virtual stranger and take off to the ends of the earth."

"It isn't as bad as it seems."

Her mother sighed expressively. She was exhausted, as Lesley could well understand. "When will I meet Chase?" was June's next question.

Lesley wasn't entirely sure. "Soon," she promised. "Listen, I got us a hotel room. You're going to need to catch your breath before we fly to Twin Creeks."

"I don't mind telling you, this felt like the longest flight of my life. I had to fly from Helena to Seattle, then wait for hours before I could get this flight." She shook her head. "I can't see you living in Alaska and liking it. You've lived in a big city all your life."

"You love Montana, don't you?"

"Yes, but that's different. Ken and I are retired."

"It isn't different at all. I've only been in Alaska for a short while and I love it already."

Her mother pinched her lips together as if to keep from saying something argumentative. "If it's all the same to you, Lesley, I'd prefer to push on. I'll rest once we reach your home and I meet this man you've married. Then and only then will I truly relax."

That posed a problem. "We can't, Mom."

"Can't do what? Meet Chase? I wondered why he wasn't here to greet me. One would think he'd be eager to meet your family. I don't imagine you've met his, either, have you?"

"Mom," Lesley said impatiently. She was troubled by the way her mother was so willing to find fault with Chase and her marriage. No doubt that was Tony's doing. Even now, he was haunting her life. More and more she'd come to realize that Tony had never really loved her. Even more enlightening was the realization that she no longer loved him. She couldn't feel as strongly as she did for Chase if she loved Tony. She missed Chase terribly.

"What?" June snapped.

"Stop trying to make Chase into

some fiend. He's not."

"You still haven't told me why he sent you to the airport by yourself," she said, in that superior way that had driven Lesley to the brink of hysteria as a teenager.

"Mother, Chase has a job. He was away on business when you called. And the reason we can't leave yet is that we can't get a flight until tomorrow."

"I will be meeting him later then?"

"Of *course.*" Lesley just wasn't sure exactly when.

They stood at the luggage carousel for several minutes until June collected her one large suitcase and her cosmetic case. Lesley took the larger of the two bags and carried it outside to the taxi line.

Her mother was worn out, and by

the time they arrived at the hotel room, Lesley was glad that Jim couldn't get them until the following morning. She was supposed to call this afternoon to confirm it.

"Would you like me to order you something to eat?" Lesley asked.

"No, thanks." June politely covered her mouth for a loud yawn. "If you don't mind, I'll lie back and just close my eyes."

"Of course I don't mind. Relax, Mom." Her mother curled up on the bed and was asleep seconds later. Lesley silently placed a sweater over June's shoulders and tiptoed to the other bed. Her intention was to read until her mother woke, but she must have fallen asleep, too, because the next thing she heard was the sound of running water.

Lesley stirred, opened her eyes and realized her mother was showering. With June occupied, Lesley reached for the phone and called Chase at both numbers. Again there was no answer at either. Discouraged, she replaced the receiver. Where could he possibly be?

"What exactly did she say?" Chase asked Jim Perkins. He found it frustrating to have this conversation by phone. Especially frustrating when he was sitting in a hotel room in Fairbanks. It would've been easier to read Jim in person. He spoke in a slow drawl and had never been one to reveal much, with either words or actions. If Chase could've talked to Jim in person, he might've been able to persuade him of the urgency of this situation.

Jim took his own sweet time answering. "She really didn't have a lot to say."

Jim was in his early forties and possessed a calm low-key attitude that had never bothered Chase before. But now he was desperate to learn everything he could about Lesley's departure from Twin Creeks.

"Surely you chatted during the flight."

"Yeah. She's the congenial sort. Personally I didn't think much of this scheme of yours of advertising for a wife, but I was wrong. Half the men in town are talking about doing something like that themselves, seeing the kind of woman you brought back with you." He paused. "I don't suppose it would work with me, though."

"What did you and Lesley talk about?" Chase asked.

"Nothing much," Jim said. "Mostly she asked about you."

"What about me?"

He seemed to need time to consider this question. "Nothin' in particular. Just how long you've lived in Twin Creeks. Things like that."

"Did she mention she was staying in a hotel?"

"She might have." Another pause. "I don't recall her saying she was, now that I think about it."

Chase had difficulty not letting his distress show. It was bad enough that Lesley had left him so soon after her arrival in Twin Creeks. But he wasn't ready to announce to the entire community that his bride of one week had deserted him. If that was true, it would come out soon enough.

"I appreciate your help, Jim. Thanks."

"I don't think you need to worry about her," Jim added in that lethargic drawl of his. "Lesley's got a good head on her shoulders. She can take care of herself."

"Yes, I know." That, however, didn't ease his mind in the least.

No sooner had he finished with the call than the phone rang. Chase grabbed it so fast, he nearly jerked the telephone off the end table. "Yes?" he snapped.

"It's Pete."

"What'd you find out?"

"Lesley's staying at the Gold Creek Hotel by the airport," came Pete's reply. "Room 204."

"How'd you learn that?" Sometimes it was better not to know where Pete got his information, but Chase couldn't help being curious.

"I've got my sources. And listen, she may be having second thoughts because she hasn't bought an airline ticket to Seattle yet. Or anywhere else."

"You're sure about that?"

"Positive." There was doubt in his voice. "Did you get any sleep last night?"

Chase closed his burning eyes. "None."

"That's what I thought. You know, Chase, if she insists on leaving, you can't make her stay."

This had been the subject of an ongoing internal debate. He didn't want to lose Lesley, but he couldn't hold her prisoner, either. If she'd decided she wanted out of his life and out of their marriage, then he couldn't stop her. Even if it meant she'd decided to return to Seattle and Tony. But he was determined to have his say before he'd let her run out on him.

"What are you going to do?" Pete asked.

"I don't know yet. I'll probably go to the hotel and see if I can talk some sense into her."

"Sounds like a good idea to me. I suppose you want to do this on your own, but if you'd like, I'll come along for moral support and wait outside."

"No, thanks, but I appreciate the offer."

"No problem. That's what friends do." Pete hesitated as if there was something more he wanted to say.

"Anything else?"

"Yeah." Again Pete hesitated. "I don't make a practice of giving advice, especially when it comes to women. My history with the opposite sex leaves a lot to be desired."

"Just say what's on your mind." Chase didn't generally seek other people's wisdom; he lived and learned by his own mistakes. This was different, though, and he was worried. He'd assumed everything was fine between them. That he could be so blind to her feelings was a shock.

"I wish now that I'd gone after Pamela," Pete said. It was the first time Chase had heard his friend say this. "I've wondered a thousand times over what would've happened if I'd taken the trouble to let her know how much I loved her, how much I needed her. If I had, she might've stayed and I wouldn't be regretting all the time that I didn't do everything I could to convince her. Don't make the same mistake."

"I don't plan on it."

"Good." Pete cleared his throat. "You love her, don't you?"

Chase wasn't sure how to answer. The physical desire they shared had overwhelmed them both. But their relationship had quickly become so much more.

When he'd first considered finding himself a wife, it had been to ease his loneliness. He was searching for a companion. A lover. A woman to keep him company during the long, dark winter months. He wanted a wife so he could bond closely with another human being. Since his parents' deaths, he'd felt detached and isolated from life.

Love had never entered into the equation. He'd never expected to fall in love this fast. Passion, yes, he'd expected that but not this kind of love.

This had been his error, Chase realized with a start. Marriage to Lesley had altered everything. Because love had come to them — or at least to him — with everything she did, everything she said. Whenever he went to bed with her, he offered her a little more of his heart. A little more of his soul. Lovemaking had become more than a physical mating, it had a spiritual aspect. He didn't know how else to describe it.

He thought about Lesley lying in bed waiting for him. She was so incredibly lovely, with her hair spilling out over the pillow . . .

It felt like a knife in his belly to think that she'd walk out on him without so much as a word.

"I do," Chase said, answering Pete's question after a profound moment. "I do love her."

"Then do whatever you have to in order to keep her," Pete advised sagely. "Even if it means leaving Twin Creeks. You can always find another job, but you may never find another Lesley."

His friend was right and Chase knew it. Now all he had to do was come up with a way of convincing Lesley to give their lives together a fighting chance.

He showered and changed clothes, flipped through the Fairbanks phone directory for the address of the Gold Creek Hotel and ordered a cab.

It would've been better if he'd been able to work out what he wanted to say, but he dared not delay a confrontation for fear he'd miss her.

Chase was grateful to Pete. His friend had said he could find Lesley through his various connections faster than Chase would be able to do it. Chase hated sitting back and letting someone else do the footwork, but in the end it had proven beneficial. Pete had located her within twelve hours.

The taxi let him off in front of the hotel. His heart was beating so hard he could hardly hear his own thoughts. Even now he didn't know what he what he was going to say.

That, however, didn't stop him from pounding at the door of room 204. When she didn't immediately answer, he knocked again, louder this time, so loud that the lady across the hall stuck her head out to see who was causing such a commotion. She threw him an irritated look and went back inside.

The door opened and Lesley stood in front of him. Suitcases sat like accusations in the background, and suddenly he was angry. He'd considered Lesley decent and honorable, not the kind of woman who'd walk out on her husband without warning.

"What do you think you're doing?" he demanded, pushing his way into the room. Lesley was so startled that she stumbled two steps back before regaining her balance.

"Chase?" She closed the door and leaned against it, her eyes wide. The perfume she wore wafted toward him. He needed every ounce of will-power not to haul her into his arms and beg her to stay with him.

"I don't understand," she said, staring at him, her eyes so innocent that the struggle not to kiss her seemed to drain his strength.

"I may have made a few mistakes along the way, but I would've thought you'd have the decency to talk to me instead of running away."

"Running away? I just flew down to Fairbanks!"

"Without a word to me," he reminded her in clipped tones.

"I left you a note." Her voice was

raised now, as well. She rested her hands on her hips and scowled at him.

"A note," he said as though he found that humorous. "What good is that when I'm here in Fairbanks?"

Lesley dropped her hands, clenching them tightly. "You didn't give me the name of the hotel where you were staying. And you didn't answer your cell. How was I *supposed* to contact you?"

Chase was embarrassed to admit that he'd left his cell phone charging and hadn't bothered to check for a message from her — because he hadn't expected one.

"So now it's my fault." Chase knew why he was arguing with her, because if he didn't, he was going to reach for her and hold her, kiss her.

"Yes, it's your fault," she cried.

"Lesley, who is this man?"

Chase whirled around to see an older woman in a bright red housecoat with matching red slippers. Her hair was wrapped in a towel.

"Mother . . ." Lesley sounded as though she was about to burst into tears. She gestured weakly toward him, before her hand fell lifelessly to her side. "This is Chase Goodman, my husband."

The woman glared at him as if he were living proof of every dreaded suspicion she'd harbored. "What's the matter with you, young man?"

"Mrs. Campbell-Sterne . . ."

"How dare you talk to Lesley like this! Have you no manners?"

Chase gave what he figured was an excellent imitation of a salmon, his mouth opening and closing sound-lessly. He looked at Lesley, desperate for her to explain, but she'd turned her back to him.

"I'm sorry," he whispered.

"As well you should be. I can tell you I had my concerns about the kind of man Lesley married. Now I can see that —"

"Would you mind if I spoke to my wife alone for a moment?" Chase interrupted. Lesley's arms were cra-dling her middle and she was staring out the window. She gave no indica-tion that she'd heard him.

"I . . . I suppose not." Mrs. Campbell-Sterne flushed. "I'll go and dress."

"Thank you," Chase said. He waited until his mother-in-law had gone into the bathroom and closed the door before he approached Lesley.

He stepped behind her and went to rest his hands on her shoulders, stopping just short. He closed his eyes briefly, then dropped his hands to his sides. "I just made a world-class jerk of myself, didn't I?"

Lesley nodded, still refusing to face him.

"You left a note at the house?"

She answered him with another sharp nod. "And messages."

"What did they say?"

"That my mother had phoned and was worried about me and our sudden marriage. She was hurt that I'd gone through with the ceremony without trying harder to contact her. She decided to fly up immediately to meet you."

"Oh . . ." He didn't know what had possessed him to think she'd leave without some kind of explanation.

"Tony called Mom and Ken," Lesley went on. "He claimed I'd married on the rebound and that I'd made a terrible mistake. He was hoping to undermine our relationship." The way Lesley said it made Chase wonder if Tony had succeeded.

After the stunt he'd just pulled, he couldn't blame Lesley for believing she *had* made a mistake. Apologies seemed grossly inadequate.

"You flew down to meet your mother." Once again he wanted to kick himself for being so stupid. No doubt her mother thought Lesley had married a madman and he'd quickly gone about proving her right.

"What's wrong with you, charging

in here like a bull moose?" Lesley demanded, finally turning to face him.

His salmon imitation returned, and he couldn't manage a word, let alone a coherent sentence.

"I'm waiting for an answer," she reminded him.

"I . . . I thought you left me," he mumbled.

"You're not serious, are you?" Her eyes, which he'd always found so bright and beautiful, were filled with disdain.

It sounded so weak. "I couldn't let you leave."

"Why not?"

Now was the perfect opportunity to confess how much he loved her, how his heart wouldn't survive without her, but he couldn't make himself say it, not with her looking at him as if he should be arrested.

"What else was I supposed to think?" he flared. "You up and left."

"You left, too, and didn't return when you said you would, but I didn't immediately leap to some outrageous conclusion."

"That's different," Chase argued, although he knew that made no sense. He disliked the turn their conversation had taken. He didn't want to quarrel; what he yearned to do was pull her into his arms, bury his face in her neck and breathe in her scent.

"Can I come out now?" June asked from the bathroom doorway. She'd changed into blue-and-green-plaid slacks and a pale blue sweater. She was nearly as tall as Lesley, with the same clear, dark, intelligent eyes. And like Lesley, her thoughts were easy to read. Chase didn't have to guess what his mother-in-law was thinking. He hadn't impressed her, nor had he done anything to reassure her that Lesley had made a wise choice in marrying him.

The worst of it was that he couldn't blame her.

"It's all right, Mom. You can come out."

"You're sure?" She said it as though she was ready to contact the police and have Chase removed.

"I'm afraid I've made a mistake," Chase said, hoping he could explain what had happened and at the same time address her concerns about his and Lesley's relationship.

"You can say that again," June

returned crisply.

"Perhaps we could discuss this over lunch." Feeding them both sounded like an excellent plan and once they were relaxed, he'd be able to smooth things over.

Lesley's mother didn't look too pleased about stepping outside the hotel room with him. She cast a guarded look in Lesley's direction. "What do you think, dear?"

"That'll be fine," Lesley said, reaching for a white sweater, neatly folded at the foot of the bed. Chase moved to help her put it on, then changed his mind. Now wasn't the time to be solicitous. Lesley wouldn't appreciate it.

Chase chose the hotel restaurant. Conversation over lunch was stilted at best. June asked him several questions, but his attention was focused on his wife. He answered June, but his gaze didn't waver from Lesley. He was hoping she'd say or do something, anything to ease his conscience.

He'd blown it. The door had been left wide open for him to explain why he'd reacted so badly. He'd been out of his mind, thinking he'd lost her.

Chase loved her. It didn't get any simpler than that. All he had to do was say it. How difficult could that be? Apparently more than he'd realized because he let the opportunity slip past.

"How long do you plan to visit?" Chase asked June, thinking ahead. He supposed he shouldn't have been so obvious, but he was already counting down the days, the hours and minutes, until he could be alone with Lesley.

"Five days," June returned stiffly. She glanced at Lesley as though to suggest that purchasing another plane ticket south would be highly advisable — for both of them.

"I was able to get the new motor this morning," Chase said to Lesley. "We can leave for Twin Creeks as soon as you're ready."

"Mother?"

"Anytime. I'm anxious to see your home, although heaven knows you haven't had much time to settle in, have you?"

"No." Lesley eyed Chase wearily.

"I'll leave you here and be back within the hour to get you," he said, reaching for the lunch tab. "Perhaps you'd care to come with me?" he asked Lesley. He tried to appear nonchalant about it, but his heart was in his throat.

"I don't think I should leave Mother," she said flatly.

Chase's shoulders fell. Her feelings couldn't have been more obvious.

Lesley couldn't remember being more furious with anyone in her life. Chase was a fool. She'd agreed to marry him, agreed to leave the life she'd made for herself, leave her friends, her career and most of her possessions, and he *still* didn't trust her. He assumed she'd walk out on him the minute his back was turned. That was what hurt so much. His lack of faith in her.

Lesley had spent the morning listing Chase's many fine qualities to her mother. By the time she'd finished, it sounded as if he were a candidate for sainthood.

Fat chance of that after the way he'd barged into their hotel room. He couldn't have shown himself in a worse light had he tried.

After Chase left, her mother was strangely silent. They sat on their beds, staring straight ahead. Every time Lesley thought of something to say, she changed her mind. Her mother would see through her efforts to make small talk in a second.

"He isn't always like this," she finally murmured.

"I certainly hope not."

"Chase is honest and hardworking."

"That remains to be seen, doesn't it?" her mother asked stiffly.

"You don't like him, do you?"

June paused. "I don't have much reason to, do I? I'm afraid you've been blinded, Lesley. How can you possibly love this man? You don't really know him . . . You couldn't. Tony said Chase disguised the truth."

"You can't trust Tony!"

"Why not? At least he called us when my own daughter hadn't bothered to let me know she was getting married. Now that I've met your husband, I can appreciate Tony's concern."

"Mother . . ."

"Hear me out, please. I've bitten my tongue for the last hour, trying not to say what I should have earlier and didn't. You have nothing in common with Chase. You might have convinced yourself that you're happy now, and that you're going to make this ridiculous marriage work, but it isn't necessary."

"Mom, please, don't." It hurt that her mother thought her marriage ridiculous. Lesley was angry with Chase all over again for having put her in this impossible situation.

"I have to speak my piece or I'll regret it the rest of my life. I made the same mistake with your father." Her voice faltered slightly. "I knew the marriage wasn't going to work, almost from the first, but I was too stubborn to admit it. I convinced myself that I was deeply in love with him. I worked hard at making the best of the situation, giving more and more of myself until there wasn't anything left to give.

"After all that, after everything I did to hold that marriage together, he walked out. To see you repeat my mistakes would be the most tragic thing that could happen to me."

Lesley felt as if she was going to break into tears. "It isn't like that with Chase and me."

"I don't believe that, not after talking to Tony and meeting Chase for myself. He isn't right for you. Anyone with a brain can see that."

"Mom . . ."

"Are you pregnant?"

"No."

Her mother sighed as though relieved. "Come back to Montana with me," June pleaded. "If you want to start over, do it there. There's always a need for good teachers. Don't make the mistakes I did, Lesley. Leave Chase now — before it's too late — and come back with me."

Lesley was so intent on listening to her mother that she didn't hear the door open. But she felt Chase's presence before she heard his words. He was studying her without emotion, without revealing a hint of his thoughts.

"Well?" he said. "Make up your mind, Lesley. What do you want to do?"

THIRTEEN

Lesley's mother was staring at her, too, pleading with her to cut her losses now.

"I . . . I thought we'd already decided to return to Twin Creeks," Lesley stammered.

June's shoulders sagged with dismay. Chase hurriedly reached for their suitcases, as though he expected Lesley to change her mind. That irritated her, too. Her mother was about to burst into tears and Chase was ignoring June completely.

The flight into Twin Creeks seemed

to take twice as long as before. Chase flew the four-seater, concentrating as hard as if he were flying an F-14 under siege. Lesley made several attempts to carry the conversation, but it became painfully obvious that neither her mother nor Chase was interested in small talk.

When they landed at the tiny airfield, Pete and Jim were there to greet them. She knew Chase had let Jim know he'd be flying them home. But she didn't understand what was going on between Pete and her husband. The minute Pete saw her, he grinned broadly and gave Chase a thumbs-up. Chase, however, didn't seem to share his friend's enthusiasm.

"This is where you live?" June asked, scowling, staring at the tundra that surrounded the town. "Why, it's . . . it's like stepping back a hundred years." The words were more accusation than comment. Lesley saw Chase's jaw tense, but he didn't say anything, which was just as well. Lesley doubted her mother would be receptive, anyway.

When they arrived at the cabin, Lesley waited curiously for her mother's reaction. June asked several questions, nodding now and then as Chase told her about his and Lesley's life in Twin Creeks. Lesley was pleased with his honest responses. She added what little information she could.

"The guest room is down the hall," Chase explained, leading them into the house. There seemed to be a détente between him and her mother, much to Lesley's relief.

June paused in the living room, staring curiously at the fireplace and the bookshelves and the desk in much the same way Lesley had earlier. Before leaving, Lesley had added several feminine touches to the house. A homemade quilt that had been her grandmother's was draped across the back of the rocking chair. A picture of her mother and Ken rested on the television and a small figurine of a harbor seal made of ash from the 1980 Mount Saint Helens eruption was propped against a Sue Grafton mystery in one of the built-in bookcases.

"This has a homey feel to it," June said grudgingly before following Chase down the narrow hallway.

Lesley bit her tongue and trailed after her mother. Already she could

see that this was going to be the longest five days of her life.

Chase was forced to wait until after
dinner before he had a chance to
speak to his mother-in-law privately.
While Lesley was busy with the dinner dishes, Chase casually suggested
a drive into town.

June hesitated, but it appeared she
had things she wanted to say to him,
too, and she agreed with a nod of her
head.

Chase walked into the kitchen.
Under normal circumstances, he
would've slipped his arms around
Lesley's waist. But these weren't
normal conditions. He was afraid of
touching her for fear of being charged
with not behaving in a circumspect
fashion. He swore his mother-in-law

had the eyes of an eagle and the temperament of a polar bear.

"Your mother and I are going for a drive," he said as casually as he could, hoping Lesley would leave it at that. He should've known better.

She hurriedly finished rinsing the pan she'd used to bake biscuits and reached for a hand towel. "I'll come with you."

"Don't be offended, but we'd both rather you didn't."

Lesley blinked and leaned against the sink. "I don't know if talking to my mother when she's in this frame of mind is a good idea."

"We either clear the air here and now, or all three of us are going to spend a miserable five days."

"But, Chase . . ."

"Honey, listen." He paused and

glanced over his shoulder. June had gone for a sweater, but would return at any moment. "You and I need to talk, too. I'm sorry about starting off on the wrong foot with your mother. I promise I'll do my best to make things right. I owe you that much — and a whole lot more."

Lesley lowered her gaze.

"I realize June's not the only one I offended," he said gruffly, walking toward her. If he didn't kiss her soon, he was going to go stark raving mad. Lesley must have felt the same way because she moved toward him, her steps as eager as his own. His heart reacted immediately, gladdened that she wanted to end this terrible tension between them.

He clasped his hands about her waist and caught her, drawing her into the shelter of his arms.

The sound of June clearing her throat behind him was like a bucket of cold water tossed over his head. He released Lesley and stepped away from her.

"We won't be long," he said, as evenly as he could.

June was fussing with her sweater when he turned around, smoothing out the sleeves. Her back was straight with unspoken disapproval. She looked prim and proper and determined to save her daughter from his nasty clutches. Chase sighed inwardly and prayed for patience.

Lesley followed them out to the front porch and watched as Chase opened the passenger door and held out his hand to help June inside. His mother-in-law ignored him and hoisted herself into the front seat.

So that was how it was going to be.

Knowing what to expect, Chase threw a look over his shoulder at Lesley and shrugged. He'd do his best, but he wasn't a miracle worker. He couldn't *force* Lesley's mother to accept him as her son-in-law, nor could he demand she give her approval to their marriage.

He climbed into the seat beside her, and started the engine. "I don't know if Lesley had a chance to tell you, but Twin Creeks is a small town," he said, as he pulled onto the dirt and gravel road. "The population is around forty."

"*Forty,*" June repeated, sounding shocked. "Did Lesley tell you she was born and raised in Seattle?"

"Yes."

"There were almost that many students in her kindergarten class. What makes you think a woman who's lived in a large populated area all her life will adjust to a place like this?"

Chase was ready for this one. "Lesley knew Twin Creeks was small when she agreed to marry me." True, she hadn't known *how* small, but she'd had the general idea.

"You haven't answered my question," June said primly, her hands tightly clasped.

"I'm hoping love will do that," he said simply.

"Aren't you asking a good deal of a woman you've only known a few weeks?"

"Yes, but —"

"It seems to me," Lesley's mother interrupted, "that neither of you has given the matter much thought. Lesley won't last a month in this primitive lifestyle."

Chase was fast losing his patience. "It seems to *me* that you don't know your daughter as well as you think you do."

"I beg your pardon," she snapped. "Do you suppose I don't realize what you did? You seduced my daughter, convinced her to marry you and then practically kidnapped her to get her to move north with you."

Chase pulled over to the side of the road. He couldn't concentrate on driving and hold on to his temper at the same time.

"Lesley mentioned that you'd spoken to Tony. I gather you're repeating what he said. Unfortunately you and I don't know each other well enough to be good judges of the other's character. You see me as some psychopath who's tricked your daughter into marriage."

"You can't blame me for that, after you charged into our hotel room, acting like a lunatic."

Chase closed his eyes with mounting frustration. When he collected himself, he continued in a calm, clear voice. "Arguing isn't going to settle anything. You believe what you must and I'll do my best to stay out of your way." He started the engine, intent on turning the vehicle around and heading back to the house. He'd tried, but hadn't lasted five minutes with June hurling accusations at him.

"Listen here, young man —"

"The last person who called me 'young man' was my junior high teacher," Chase retorted. "I'm a long way from junior high, so I suggest you either call me by name or keep quiet."

She gasped indignantly, and Chase wondered how it was possible to love Lesley so much, yet feel so negative toward her mother.

"What you fail to understand," he said, after a lengthy pause, "is that we have something in common."

"I sincerely doubt that."

"We both love Lesley."

"Yes, but —"

"There aren't any qualifiers as far as I can see," he interrupted. "She's your daughter, the woman you've raised and nurtured and loved all these years. I don't have the same history with Lesley, but I love her. Right now those may be only words to you, but I'd rather die than hurt her. If your main concern is that she won't adjust to life here in Alaska, then let me assure you, we'll move."

"This all sounds very convenient. You're telling me what I want to hear."

"I'm telling you the truth." His anger flared briefly, then died down just as quickly. "We were wrong not to make more of an effort to contact you about the wedding. If you want to blame someone for that, then I'll accept the guilt. I was in a hurry —"

"You rushed her into making a decision."

Chase had another argument poised and ready, but he'd recognized early on that there was nothing he could say that would alter June's opinion of him.

"I don't think we're going to be able to talk this out," he said, not bothering to disguise his disappointment. "I'd never keep Lesley here against her will, that much I promise you. You've raised a wonderful woman and I love her more than my own life. I can't offer you any greater reassurance than that."

His words were greeted with silence.

"You and your husband will always be welcome here, especially after we start our family."

She turned and glared at him as if he'd said something offensive, but Chase was tired of trying to decipher this woman's thoughts.

"If Lesley wants to visit you and your husband in Montana, she can go with my blessing," he added. It went without saying that *he* wouldn't be welcome. "I apologize for making an idiot of myself earlier. I don't blame you for thinking ill of me, but I'd hoped we'd be able to put that behind us and start again. Perhaps before you leave, we'll be able to do that." He switched gears, turned the vehicle around and drove back to the house.

Lesley was knitting in the rocking chair when he walked inside. She glanced up anxiously, but must have read the defeat in his eyes, and the disdain in her mother's, because she sagged against the back of the chair.

"What are you knitting?" June asked, revealing some enthusiasm for the first time in hours.

"A sweater for Chase. One of the ladies in town sells yarn, so while I was there I picked up a pattern and everything else I was going to need."

"You met Thelma?" Chase asked, claiming the recliner next to his wife.

"I had tea with all the ladies," Lesley informed him. She was trying not to smile. Her mouth quivered and the need to kiss her felt nearly overwhelming.

So she'd gone into town on her own. Chase should've realized she was too anxious to meet the others to wait for him to introduce her.

"It's stuffy in here," June announced.

"There's a chair on the porch," Chase suggested. If his curmudgeon of a mother-in-law wasn't standing guard over them, he might be able to steal a few minutes alone with his wife.

"I think I'll sit out there for a while."

"Good idea," Chase said with just a smidgen of glee. To his credit, he didn't lock the door behind her.

"What happened?" Lesley asked in a breathy whisper the instant her mother was out the door.

"She thinks I seduced you into moving up here with me."

Lesley batted her long lashes at him. "You did, didn't you?"

"I'd certainly like the opportunity to do so again," he said, waggling his brows suggestively. "I'm not going to last another five days without making love to you. Maybe not even another five minutes —"

"Chase!" Lesley whispered, as he moved toward her. "My mother's right outside."

"She already thinks I'm a sex fiend as it is."

"You are!"

Chase chuckled, but his humor was cut short by a piercing scream from the front porch. Never in his life had Chase moved faster. Lesley reacted just as quickly. Her knitting needles and yarn flew toward the ceiling as they both raced out the front door.

June was backed against the front of the house, her hands flattened over her heart. Even from several feet away, Chase could see she was trembling.

"What happened?" he demanded.

June closed her eyes and shook her head. Luckily Lesley was there to comfort her. She wrapped her arms around her mother and gently guided her toward the door.

"Something must have frightened her," Chase said. He debated going for his hunting rifle, then decided against it. Whatever the danger had been, it'd passed.

"It was . . . huge." The words were strangled-sounding.

"A bear, Mom. Did you see a bear?" Lesley's eyes widened with fear, but her mother shook her head.

"It must've been a moose," Chase speculated. He recalled the first time he'd come nose to nose with one. It was an experience he'd rather not repeat.

"No." June shook her head again.

"A wolf?" Lesley pressed.

"No," his mother-in-law moaned. Lesley led her into the house and urged her down in the rocker while Chase went for a glass of water.

"It was a . . . a *spider*," June said, gripping the glass with both hands. "A black one with long legs. I . . . I've never liked spiders."

Judging by June's reaction, that was an understatement.

"A spider?" Chase whispered. The woman had sounded as though she'd barely escaped with her life.

His wife shrugged and rolled her eyes.

"Suggest she go to bed and rest," he said in hushed tones.

Lesley's lips quivered with the effort it took to suppress a smile.

"Maybe you'd better lie down," Lesley said in a soothing voice.

"You're right," June murmured, clearly shaken by the encounter. "I don't usually overreact like this. It's just that this spider was so *big*. I didn't expect there to be spiders here in Alaska, of all places."

"We all have a tendency to over-react under certain circumstances," Chase said, using the opportunity to defend his own behavior earlier in the day. "Later we realize how foolish we must have looked to everyone else. People generally understand and forgive that sort of thing." As far as sermons went, he felt he'd done well. He was no TV evangelist, but he figured he'd got his point across. He only hoped June had picked up on his message.

"I do feel like I should rest."

"I'll check out the room first," Chase offered, "and make sure there's nothing there." All he needed was for June to interrupt him and Lesley. He didn't know how well his heart would stand up to another bloodcurdling scream.

"Thank you," June whispered as he hurried out.

When he came back to signal that all was clear, Lesley accompanied her mother to the bedroom. After five minutes Chase was glancing at his watch, wondering how long this was going to take.

Another ten minutes passed before Lesley returned to the living room. "Mom's resting comfortably. I gave her a couple of aspirin to settle her nerves."

"I need something to settle my nerves, too," Chase said, reaching for her and pulling her onto his lap.

"Chase." She put up a token struggle.

"Kiss me."

"I . . . I don't think that's a good idea."

"Considering what I *really* want, a kiss seems darn little. Don't be stingy, Lesley, I need you." If they'd been alone, he'd have had her in bed fifteen seconds after they got home. As it was, he'd been forced to sit through an uncomfortable dinner and then deal with her dragon of a mother before and after the spider attack. A kiss was small compensation.

He nibbled at her ear. He'd settle for kissing her. It was all he wanted right now, just enough to satisfy him until he could tell her all that was in his heart.

He could feel her resistance, the little there was, melt away.

She turned her head until their lips

met. The kiss was slow and deep. It demanded every shred of stamina he had to drag his mouth away from hers. By then, Lesley's arms had circled his neck and she was sighing softly. She laid her head on his shoulder and worked her fingers into his hair.

Now was the time to tell her. He forced his mind from the warmth of her body pressing against his, her moist breath fanning his neck.

"When I spoke to your mother . . ." The words wouldn't come. Maybe this would be easier after they'd made love.

"Yes?" Lesley lifted her head, curiosity brightening her eyes.

"I told her something I've never told you." Their eyes met and her mouth widened with an enticing smile.

"I love you, Lesley." There it was, out in the open for her to accept or reject. His heart was there, too, along with his dreams for their future.

Lesley tensed, her hands on his shoulders. "What did you just say?" Her voice was barely audible.

"I love you." It sounded so naked, saying it like that. "I realize blurting it out might make you uncomfortable, but I didn't think it was fair if I told your mother how I felt and said nothing to you."

She was off his lap in a flash. Tears glazed her eyes as she backed away from him.

"I was sure of it when I thought you'd left me," he explained. "I'd tried to reach you by phone and when I couldn't, I had Pete go to the cabin. He told me the truck was gone and that Jim had flown you into Fairbanks. I didn't know what to think. Now it seems ludicrous to leap to the conclusions I did, but at the time it made perfect sense."

"I see." One tear escaped the corner of her eye and rolled down the side of her face.

"Say something," he pleaded. His heart was precariously perched at the end of his sleeve. The least she could do was let him know if she was about to pluck it off and crush it beneath her feet.

"I knew when we got married that you didn't love me," she said, without looking at him. "When we were in Victoria — I knew you didn't love me then, either."

"Don't be so sure," he returned, frowning. He understood the problem, had always understood it. Tony. She was in love with her former fiancé and that wasn't likely to change for a long time.

Her head snapped up. "You were in love with me on our honeymoon?"

He shrugged, unwilling to reveal everything quite so soon. He wished she'd express her feelings for him.

"Were you?" she asked again.

Chase stood and rubbed his hand along the back of his neck, walking away from her. "Does it matter?"

"Yes."

"All right," he muttered. "As near as I can figure, I loved you when we got married. It just took me a while to . . . put everything together." He shoved his hands inside his pockets. This wasn't going as well as he'd hoped.

"I tried to reassure your mother, but that didn't work," he continued. "Tony's got her convinced you married me on the rebound and that it was a mistake."

"I didn't."

Now it was Chase's turn to go still. He was afraid to believe what he thought she was saying.

"You *aren't* in love with Tony?" he asked breathlessly.

"That would be impossible when I'm crazy in love with you." She smiled then, the soft womanly smile that never failed to stir him. Her love shone like a beacon.

Chase closed his eyes to savor her words, to wrap them around his heart and hold on to the feeling. It happened then, a physical need, a craving for her that was so powerful it nearly doubled him over.

They moved toward each other, their kisses fuel to the flames of their desire.

"Chase," Lesley groaned between kisses, unbuttoning his shirt as she spoke. "We can't. . . . Mother's room is directly down the hall from us. She'll hear."

Chase kissed her while trying to decide what to do.

"The cache," he said, grateful for the inspiration. It wasn't the ideal solution, but it would serve their purpose.

Lesley's legs seemed to have given out on her and he lifted her into his arms, pausing only long enough to grab the quilt from the rocking chair.

He gathered her in his arms, holding her close with a fierce possessiveness.

"I love you." Each time he said it, the words came more easily.

"I know." She spread a slow series of kisses along his jaw.

"Your mother . . ."

"Don't worry about Mom. She'll come around, especially when she's got grandchildren to spoil."

"Children," Chase said softly.

"Is this a new concept to you?"

"Not entirely." He grinned and she smiled back.

"Good." Her teeth caught his lower lip. "Soon I hope," she said a moment later.

"How soon?"

Lesley raised her head and her beautiful dark eyes gazed down at him. "No time like the present, is there?"

Chase sucked in his breath. He'd thought they'd wait a year, possibly longer, to start their family, but he couldn't refuse Lesley anything.

"Will I ever grow tired of you?" he wondered aloud.

"Never," she promised.

Chase instinctively knew it was true.

EPILOGUE

"Grandma, Grandma." Three-year-old Justin Goodman tore out of Lesley's grasp as they stepped into the small airport and he ran into the waiting arms of June Campbell-Sterne.

June hugged her grandson and lifted him from the ground. "Oh, my, you've gotten so big."

Justin's chubby arms circled his grandmother's neck and he squeezed tightly.

"Justin's not the only one who's grown," Chase said, slipping his arm around Lesley's thickened waist.

"You would have, too, if you were about to have a baby," Lesley reminded her husband.

Chase chuckled and shook hands with Ken Sterne.

"Good to see you again," Ken said. "June's been cooking for three days. You'd think an army was about to descend on us."

"Hush now," June chastised her husband. "How are you feeling?"

Lesley sighed. How did any woman feel two months before her delivery date? Anxious. Nervous. Eager. "I'm okay."

June put down her grandson and kissed Chase on the cheek.

His eyes met Lesley's and he gave her a know-it-all look. It had taken time, but Lesley had been right about the effect grandchildren would have on the relationship between her mother and her husband. When they'd first met, four years earlier, her mother had been convinced Chase was some kind of demon. These days he was much closer to sainthood.

"How's Twin Creeks?" Ken asked, steering the small party toward the baggage area.

"The population has doubled," Lesley informed him proudly. It had started soon after her arrival. Pete had gotten married the following spring and he and his wife already had two children and another on the way. Even Jim had married, which surprised them all. A widow with four children had found a place in all their hearts.

It seemed there was a baby being born every few months. The community was thriving. Lesley believed Chase was the one who'd put everything in motion; his venture into Seattle to find himself a wife was what had started the process. Soon the other men working at the pump station were willing to open their lives.

Chase, however, was convinced that once the other men saw what a wonderful woman *he'd* found, they'd decided to take their chances, as well.

Whatever the reason, there were fifteen more women residing in Twin Creeks. Ten of them had apparently made it a personal goal to populate Alaska.

She placed one arm around her husband and smiled softly to herself.

How different her life would have been without him. Each and every day she thanked God for that crazy billboard she'd seen on her way to the store.

BRIDE WANTED.

Their marriage was meant to be — because he'd chosen her although she hadn't answered his ad. And he'd let her know in a million ways since that *she* was the bride he wanted.

We hope you have enjoyed this Large Print book. Other Thorndike, Wheeler, Kennebec, and Chivers Press Large Print books are available at your library or directly from the publishers.

For information about current and upcoming titles, please call or write, without obligation, to:

Publisher
Thorndike Press
10 Water St., Suite 310
Waterville, ME 04901
Tel. (800) 223-1244

or visit our Web site at:

http://gale.cengage.com/thorndike

OR

Chivers Large Print
published by AudioGO Ltd
St James House, The Square
Lower Bristol Road
Bath BA2 3SB
England
Tel. +44(0) 800 136919
email: info@audiogo.co.uk
www.audiogo.co.uk

All our Large Print titles are designed for easy reading, and all our books are made to last.